I0675853

# The Best Man

## PAT BALLARD

PEARLSONG PRESS
NASHVILLE, TN

Pearlsong Press
P.O. Box 58065
Nashville, TN 37205
www.pearlsong.com
1-866-4-A-PEARL

ISBN-13: 978-1-59719-010-7
Library of Congress Control Number: 2007924061

Original trade paperback

Cover design by Zelda Pudding

Other books by Pat Ballard published by Pearlsong Press:

*Dangerous Curves Ahead: Short Stories*
*Wanted: One Groom*
*Nobody's Perfect*
*His Brother's Child*
*A Worthy Heir*
*Abigail's Revenge*

To all my loyal readers:
Thank you.

# Chapter 1

**"That's it!" Lana muttered.** The crumpled wad of paper flew from her hand and landed dead center in the wastebasket a few feet away, validating her decision. "No more diets! I won't spend the rest of my life hungry. If my body hasn't gotten skinny from eighteen years of dieting and being hungry, then it's just not going to get skinny. So forget about it."

The empty room didn't argue with her, but she knew it would be a different story when she spoke those same words out loud to her sister, Jenny. An entirely different story.

But she didn't care. She was tired of the never-ending battle of trying to stay a size that her body kept trying to tell her wasn't natural. Tired of obsessing every day over what she could and couldn't eat, fearing if she ate the wrong thing it would show up on the scales the next day. "Damn those scales, anyway," she spoke to the room again. And soon the bathroom scales made a loud metallic thump into the same wastebasket, on top of the crumpled diet plan that she'd just this morning printed off the Internet.

Briskly brushing her hands together, as if to end the subject right here and now, Lana picked up the wastebasket and carried the offending objects that it held to the outside dumpster before she had time to change her mind.

Back in her living room, she was overcome with a simultaneous fear and elation. *FREEDOM!* part of her brain shouted. *But what if you get so fat you can't get out of the house?* the other part of her brain argued.

"I'll deal with that if it happens," she admonished the empty, listening room. "I'll eat anything I want, in moderation—well, unless I want to pig out occasionally—I'll exercise when I can, and we're just going to see what happens. So all you little voices in my head go take a hike!"

**The moment of truth came sooner than she'd expected,** later that day when she got a call from her mom asking her to come over for dinner. Her younger sister, Jenny, and Jenny's fiancé were going to be there, and they needed to talk about their wedding plans.

"Lana, what are you doing?" Jenny's horrified voice squeaked as Lana placed a piece of lemon icebox pie on her dessert plate. They'd finished the wonderful meal their mother had prepared and were about to have the dessert she'd made.

"I'm doing the same thing you're doing, Jenny," Lana answered, looking pointedly at the pie on Jenny's plate. "I'm having dessert."

"But you know you'll gain weight if you eat that. I can get by with it, but you can't."

"So just because I inherited Dad's genes to gain weight easily, I have to do without all the good stuff? Well, not anymore, little sister. I made up my mind today that I'm finished with dieting. I'm going to live a little."

"But Lana—"

"Don't whine, Jenny," Alma, their mom, interjected. "Lana, honey, I'm so happy to hear you say that. I've been worried about your health for a long time. A person can starve their body for just so long without doing real damage to it." Alma was a dietitian at a local hospital and knew that Lana didn't eat a balanced diet.

"But Mom! What about the dresses we're having made? What if she gets so fat she can't fit into her maid of honor dress?"

"Excuse me? Hello? I'm still in the room, Jenny. If I outgrow my dress in six months, then I'll have a larger one made. It's just that simple."

"But there's a time factor, Lana. If the dresses get made and you outgrow yours, there won't be time to make another one," Jenny persisted.

"Then I'll wear my jogging pants and tennis shoes," Lana answered, growing tired of the discussion.

Jenny knew when her older sister was getting angry, so she approached the subject from another direction. "How does Ron feel about this?" she asked, referring to the man Lana had been dating for about a year.

"He doesn't know yet. Like I said, I've just made the decision today."

"How do you think he'll feel?" Jenny pushed.

"You know, Sis, I don't really care how he feels. I've decided that it's time in my life to do what feels right to me and let the other people around me either accept me for who I really am or just stay away from me."

Hank, Jenny's fiancé, sat quietly beside her and listened to the women's conversation. Personally, he wished Jenny would put on a few pounds. He loved her, but he sure wouldn't care if she were a little larger. A smile toyed with the corners of his mouth, just thinking about a plumper Jenny.

His ringing cell phone interrupted his fantasy. "Sorry," he said to the table of arguing women, then answered the phone. "Sure, you're on the right street. Just come on down three houses on the left, and you'll see my car."

"Was that Tony?" Jenny asked.

"Yes, he's just down the street," Hank answered.

"Tony?" Lana asked.

"Tony has been my best friend since we were in first grade," Hank said. He's the best man in the wedding. He's coming by to discuss the wedding plans with us."

*Good*, Lana thought. Maybe the diversion would get Jenny off the weight topic.

"In fact," Hank spoke up again, "Tony is the best man for about anything that could happen in life. He's always been there for me. I'm closer to him than I am my blood brother. He's—here he is now," he finished, getting up to go answer the ringing doorbell.

"Lana, will you just give this some more thought?" Jenny started in again. "I'm only concerned for your own health. You know how unhealthy being overweight is."

"Jenny, let's just drop the subject for tonight, okay?" Alma stepped in. "And besides that, it's never actually been proven that being a larger size is unhealthy. Lifestyle is the main factor in health."

"Ladies, this is Tony," Hank spoke from the dining room doorway.

Tony was not what Lana had expected. She wasn't sure exactly what she'd expected, but it wasn't the man she was looking at. He looked to be a little less than six feet tall, and was of average build, not a big man at all. But his presence—his very energy filled the small dining room, making it seem to have suddenly shrunk. Jet-black hair waved back from a wide forehead, confirming the look of great intelligence that shone from his honey-brown eyes as they met and held Lana's. A feathering of gray at the temples seemed to accentuate those intense eyes.

"Of course you've met Jenny, and this is Lana, Jenny's sister, and their mother, Alma." Hank made the introductions.

Lana hypnotically watched the smile cross Tony's perfect mouth as he nodded to them and said, "Hello, ladies, the pleasure is mine."

*Not even close*, Lana thought. *The pleasure is all mine!* Aloud she said, "It's nice to meet you, Tony."

"Come have some coffee and pie," Alma invited, sliding out a chair directly across from Lana.

The dining table seated eight people comfortably, but it suddenly felt only large enough for two. Tony's aura reached out and enveloped Lana. She'd never been this aware of another human being. Much less, a man.

"Lana is the maid of honor," Hank said.

"If she can fit in the dress by then," Jenny muttered.

"Jenny, honey, why don't we just let this drop for the night," Hank softly admonished Jenny.

But it seemed that Jenny's mind was made up to cause a scene.

"I don't want to let it drop, Hank. We can't let this crazy thought of hers take root overnight. We have to talk some sense into her head right now.  Knowing her, she can gain five pounds from that one piece of pie she's eating."

"Jenny!" Alma scolded. She set Tony's coffee down and handed him a dessert plate  with pie before continuing. "Jenny, that is enough on this subject for tonight." Finality sounded in every word.

"Actually, Mom, now that we have Tony's curiosity up, I'll explain to him what's in Jenny's craw. Then maybe we can get on with talking about the wedding."

"Well," Jenny pouted, "this subject is about the wedding, too."

"You're absolutely right," Lana agreed. "It *is* your wedding, and I understand that you want everything perfect. And I promise you that I'm not going to do anything to ruin your beautiful wedding." Turning back to Tony, she explained, "I've made an announcement tonight that has upset Jenny. I've decided to stop dieting, and Jenny's afraid I'm going to get too fat for my maid of honor dress."

There. It was out in the open. Now that he knew she would soon be fat, she wouldn't have to worry about him being attracted to her, not that she thought he would be, anyway.

Tony held Lana's gaze momentarily before his face split in a huge grin. Turning to Jenny, he said, "Jenny, my dear, I, as the best man, promise you that if Lana outgrows the dress you're having made, then I'll pay for having one made that fits her at the time of the wedding. In fact, before I leave tonight, give me a small sample of the material and I'll order some into the store to have in stock just in case we need to make another dress. I have in-store tailors who can whip out a dress in twenty-four hours, if necessary. Does that make you feel better?"

"See what I mean?" Hank broke in. "This man can make anything okay."

"Hold on, friend." Tony fastened Hank with sad eyes. "We both know there are a few things that I couldn't fix."

"Oh, thank you, Tony." Jenny's mood suddenly changed and her world was temporarily okay. "Owning Angelino's Department store would let you do what you're talking about, huh?" Suddenly she didn't seem so worried about Lana's health.

"Angelino's?" Lana's azure blue eyes grew large. Angelino's was the swankiest department store in the area.

"Anthony Angelino, at your service, m'lady." Tony extended his hand with an exaggerated bow over the table.

Lana automatically extended her hand and felt it swallowed in his large one. He might not be a big man, but he sure had big hands, she realized, looking down at the tanned hand that engulfed her smaller pale one.

"You have lovely hands," he surprised her by saying, as he turned her hand over in his and lifted it to his lips, briefly brushing the back with a light kiss.

"Alright, already! Let's talk wedding," Jenny said impatiently. The attention had been off her for too long.

"Yes, let's," Lana agreed, reluctantly withdrawing her hand from Tony's, but still mesmerized by his steady gaze.

**After two hours of planning, debating, note-taking** and easy banter, Alma leaned back in her chair and said, "I don't know about the rest of you, but I'm ready for a break."

"That sounds like a great idea," Tony said, reaching for the pie plate. "Would you like to split a piece with me?" he asked Lana.

Did she just imagine the mischievous look he flashed her or was it real? "Sure," she answered his challenging look.

"Oh, great. Now he's going to feed her," Jenny mumbled, supposedly for Hank's ears only, but the entire room heard her.

Tony placed a slice of pie on his dessert plate, then meticulously cut it in half. When he was finished, he took his fork and dipped up a bite and lifted it to her mouth. A challenge mingled with pure devilment gleamed in his eyes, daring her to defy her sister's sarcastic remark.

Deliberately, Lana slowly licked her full heart-shaped lips before opening them to take the treat offered to her.

Tony watched her lips close over the pie and slide it slowly off the fork. Felt the tremor of desire in his lower body, and knew he was in trouble.

**Two weeks later, as Lana put on her favorite pair of jeans,** she realized they were getting a little snug. It had started. But she'd known it would. If she weren't hungry all the time, then she *would* gain weight. And she would gain it quickly. She could gain five or ten pounds in a couple of weeks.

Her throat felt tight as panic rose inside her. Her first impulse was to run to the closest supermarket and purchase the latest magazine with the newest weight-loss miracle on the front of it.

"No!" she said aloud. She'd made up her mind to stop the craziness of self-starvation, and she would stick with it!

She'd get in the attic at her mom's house this week, and pull out her boxes of fat clothes. The basics like jeans, and some of the slacks and tops, would still be in style from two years ago when she'd slipped off her diet and spent a fat year.

But what if she gained even more than she usually did when she fell off the diet wagon?

"I'll deal with it if it happens," she spoke to her reflection in the mirror as she put the final touches on her shoulder-length black hair before heading out the door to meet Ron for lunch. The cool, yet balmy April breeze tousled her hair, reminding her that Mobile Bay was only a few miles away. A few fluffy white clouds sailed across the blue skies imitating the sailboats that she loved to watch out in the bay.

"Hi, babe," Ron said, standing and kissing Lana on the cheek when she got to the restaurant. "You look beautiful, as usual," he said as he pulled her chair out for her.

"Thank you. And you look quite dashing yourself," she answered.

Ron always looked like a model who had just stepped out of a man's magazine. His blond hair and sky-blue eyes were the icing on the cake of his buff body. He worked out faithfully, and it showed.

The waiter appeared and took their order. When he left, Ron looked quizzically at Lana. "You usually just order a salad for lunch."

"I know. But I'm tired of spending my days hungry. So, today I'm having a chicken sandwich with my salad."

"You've done so well with your diet this year, I'd just hate to see you blow it," Ron said, with just a hint of censorship in his voice.

Ron and Lana had met just as she was getting back on her last diet. She was starting to lose weight when he first asked her out. They'd been dating ever since, and he'd been very supportive and complimentary at her progress. Lana was curious as to how he was going to react to her new decision.

"I'm tired of dieting, Ron. I'm tired of being hungry all day, every day. I'm tired of obsessing over food. What to eat or what not to eat. Mostly, what not to eat."

"You've never mentioned this before," he said quietly.

"I know. But it's been on my mind a lot lately. So I made the decision a couple of weeks ago to stop dieting. That doesn't mean that I'm not going to take care of my health. I'll eat healthily, within a non-obsessive range, and I'll exercise moderately. Again, I'm not going to be obsessive-compulsive about any of this, anymore. I want to spend my brainpower on more creative subjects than food. And I want to have enough energy to get through my days without feeling so tired and wasted."

"So how big do you think you'll get?" Concern edged his voice.

"I have no idea," Lana answered. "But Ron, I want you to know that you're free to leave this relationship if you're not comfortable with my weight gain."

There! She'd said it, and it was very easy to say. Maybe that answered her question as to whether she loved him or not.

"Then you're saying that you care more about food than me." Disappointment sounded in his voice.

"I'm saying that I care more about my health than I do about staying slim. It really has nothing to do with my feelings toward you. But if you're asking if I'm willing to be hungry for you, then the answer is no."

"I thought that was what love was all about. Sacrificing for the one you love."

"In other words, if I love you, I'll be willing to stay hungry all day, every day, to prove it? Just to look a certain way?"

"Sure. That's what we do for each other. I work out to stay in shape for you."

"Ron, be honest, here. You worked out long before you and I met. You work out for yourself, and that's a good thing. All I'm saying is that if you love someone, you'd never ask them to do anything that is harmful to them, just to prove their love, or to look like you want them to look."

"But I do love you."

"Then you'll love me at whatever my real size is. Because that will be the real me."

"But I love the you that you are now. I don't know if I'll love the fat you."

"Ron! Listen to yourself. What you're saying is you love my body. *This* is the real me," Lana said, pointing to her head and her heart. "My mind and my soul. That's the real me. My body is just the package that the real me is wrapped in. If you just love my body, then you don't love *me*."

The waiter set their salads in front of them, and Ron lavishly poured blue cheese dressing on his, then almost gasped when Lana did the same. She usually had no dressing, or used a little of the oil and vinegar house dressing.

Seeing Ron's surprised look, Lana remembered the night at her mom's house and Tony's deliberate taunting of Jenny, and her mischievous spirit kicked in. She licked her lips with relish as she tasted her first bite. "This salad dressing is heavenly, isn't it?" she remarked innocently.

"Yeah, it's pretty good," Ron acknowledged reluctantly.

But when the waiter brought their meal and Lana took her first bite of the chicken sandwich, the look on Ron's face was almost contemptuous. Suddenly Lana didn't feel mischievous. She felt resentment. While Ron eagerly began to eat his steak and potato, he wanted her to be content with a salad with barely any dressing on it.

"Ron, you might as well get used to seeing me eat. If you can't deal with it, then you need to make a decision about it. I'm not going to live my life with you standing in constant judgment of me. I know this is new to you, so I'll forgive your reactions today. But you need to take a week away from me and make a decision."

And she put her napkin on the table and quietly walked out of the restaurant.

**Sitting in her car, she fumed.** How dare Ron look at her as if she'd sprouted two heads! She'd wondered how he would react if she regained her weight after they were married, or after she'd had a child. She thought she had her answer today. Thank *God* she'd found out before she got married.

*But give him a chance to decide,* the voice of reason echoed in her head.

Well, after that look today, she had a feeling the decision was already made.

# Chapter 2

**Lana was busy at her desk** at the See the World travel agency when she heard the melodic tinkling indicating someone was coming through the door. She looked up into the warm eyes of Tony Angelino.

"The beautiful Lana Clarke," he said, approaching her desk.

"The handsome Tony Angelino," she answered in kind.

"I didn't know you worked here, until today," he said, making himself at home in one of the plush leather chairs in front of her desk.

"I've been here for five years."

"Hmmm. Then I've been using the wrong travel agency. I knew there was a reason I decided to come here today." His eyes held hers and she felt as if she were being pulled toward him.

"Where do you want to go?" Lana asked, shaking herself loose from his hypnotic gaze.

"To lunch with you," he answered, not taking his eyes from her.

"Okay. Then where?" She had to concentrate in order to form a coherent sentence.

"It depends on how lunch goes," he answered, winking at her.

Lana knew he was just flirting with her, but she felt her pulse racing anyway. He'd turned the magnetism up since the night at her mom's. She wondered why.

"Actually, I need to book a two-week's package to the Bahamas," Tony said, sensing, to his surprise, that the woman in front of him was actually blushing at his teasing. What an intriguing concept in this day and age. Sexy as all get out, yet acted as if she didn't even know it. And blushing, on top of that. Nobody could fake a blush!

"When do you need this?"

"By the end of next week, if possible. I know this is short notice, but I was told by a friend that your agency was known for pulling off the impossible."

"And who was this friend that gave us such high ratings?" Lana asked.

"Your mom."

"My mom?" Her eyes flew to his. "Since when have you and my mom become friends?"

"Since that first night I came over to talk about Jenny's wedding. Your mom is a wonderful woman."

Lana looked at Anthony Angelino more closely. She knew he must be several years older than her, but surely too young to be dating her mom. Although her mom was only nineteen years older than she was. So if Tony were ten years older than her, he'd only be nine years younger than her mom—so it was possible. But she couldn't believe her mom was already dating. Her dad had only been dead a year.

Lana missed her father dreadfully, but knew how lonely her mom had been since his death, so she wouldn't mind if she was dating someone. It would take her mind off her loneliness.

"Hello? Where did you go? I've lost you." Tony's teasing voice brought Lana's attention back to him.

"Oh. I'm sorry. Were you saying something?"

"I said your mom is a wonderful woman."

"Yes, I heard that. And I agree. She is. And I love her very much, so you'd better not hurt her."

"Excuse me?"

"If you two are dating, I hope your intentions are good, because I don't want to see my mom hurt. Dad has only been dead for a year, and Mom's very lonely and vulnerable right now. So don't you dare break her heart!" Lana ended passionately.

She wasn't expecting his sudden outburst of laughter. "Lana, don't get me wrong. Your mom's a very attractive woman, but she's not my type."

"Really?" Lana wondered how any man could say that about her mother. Her mom was very young-acting and -looking for her age. She was everything Lana wasn't. Alma was naturally tall, slim and blond, with blue eyes that could stop you dead in your tracks. Lana had her mom's eyes, but Jenny got the rest of their mom's looks. Jenny had always been a tall, slim, natural blonde. Lana looked like her dad and his family. The Clarkes had dark hair and olive skin, and a lot of them were heavy. "Thick," as they referred to themselves, jokingly.

"Really." Tony's eyes held hers as he answered. "So now that we have that settled, where do you want to go for lunch?"

"You're serious about going to lunch?"

"Yes. I'm serious. Can you leave the office? It's almost noon. I'm assuming you do get a lunch break?"

"Yes. Carmen is in the back office doing paperwork. I'll tell her I'm going. But we need to book your trip for next week, first."

"We can do that when we get back. Let's find a place to eat before the lunch-bunch gets there. Do you like Italian food?"

"Love it!" Lana answered with gusto.

"Great. Let Carmen know you're leaving. I know the perfect place."

**After telling Carmen she was going to lunch,** Lana found herself sitting in Tony's Mercedes as he maneuvered it through traffic.

"Why?" Lana asked. Why did Anthony Angelino want to take her to lunch?

"Why what?" he asked.

Lana glanced quickly at him. Had she spoken her question out loud? Apparently she had, as Tony sat waiting for an answer.

"Why do you want to take me to lunch?"

"Why not? You're a beautiful woman, and I'm a man who appreciates a beautiful woman. So why not?"

Lana had never considered herself beautiful. She knew she wasn't mud-duck ugly, but beautiful? During her fat periods she didn't even consider herself pretty. Jenny was the pretty one. That's what everyone said when they were growing up. Everyone referred to Lana as the sweet, friendly one, and Jenny as the pretty one.

"So why not, Lana? I answered your question, now you answer mine."

She was caught in the trap of her own mouth. Which wasn't all that uncommon. She was also known as the one who would speak her mind. Her dad always told her she said what other people were thinking but were afraid to say.

"Well—first, thank you for the compliment. I've never considered myself beautiful, so thank you. And second, we've only met once. I'm definitely not in the Angelinos league of society, so I just don't understand why you would ask me to lunch. Unless, of course, you wanted to talk about the wedding." Suddenly she felt stupid. Of course that's what it was. He was the best man and she was the maid of honor, so he probably wanted to talk to her about the wedding. And she'd made a fool of herself assuming he wanted to take her to lunch for social reasons.

"Nope. Don't want to talk about the wedding. I just want to have lunch with a woman who makes my blood boil. And you, beautiful Lana, make my blood run very hot. Also, you can get used to being called beautiful, because you are. I don't know why you'd think otherwise. And last, but not least, I didn't know the Angelinos had a league of society. Is that like a baseball league?" He reached over and took her hand and kissed the back of it. "Just relax and let's enjoy a good meal and each other's company, okay?"

"Okay," she responded over the loud pounding of her heart. But she couldn't shake the feeling that Tony was just playing a game with her.

He headed into the ritzy part of town she didn't frequent very often. Soon he pulled into a side street and stopped in front of a modest little place named Alfonzo's. Immediately a young woman in a uniform came forward to park the car.

*Small but swanky*, Lana thought as Tony opened her door to help her out of the car.

It was obvious that he was well known as soon as they walked into the place. Waiters and waitresses waved and smiled at him, and a man in a suit approached them with a big smile.

"Tony! You've brought a beauty queen with you this time," he said with a heavy Italian accent.

"Alfonzo, this is Lana." Tony introduced her after giving the man a warm hug.

Alfonzo took Lana's hand and lifted it to his lips in a gallant kiss. "Thank you for gracing our humble establishment with your beauty," he gushed, then led them to a table. After seating them and bantering with Tony a few more minutes, they were left alone.

"See, Alfonzo thinks you're beautiful, too."

"It must be an Italian thing," she said, trying to play Alfonzo's lavish compliments off. "This is nice," she added, glancing around at the Italian old-country décor. She felt as if she'd been transported to a different time and place.

"Alfonzo's has been here for many years," Tony said. "Alfonzo's father initially started this restaurant when Alfonzo was a small boy. His dad named the restaurant after him."

Just then the waiter came up and set a basket of heavenly smelling fresh-baked bread on the table. He set an empty plate down and poured olive oil into it, and lavishly sprinkled herbs over the oil. After he'd finished, he asked if he could take their drink order.

"Actually, we'll go ahead and order everything now," Tony said.

Lana frantically searched the menu. She liked Italian food, but didn't know that much about it, and didn't recognize anything except lasagna and spaghetti on the menu.

"Would you like for me to order for you?" Tony asked.

"Yes!" Lana said with relief.

Tony ordered two sampler plates and a bottle of red wine.

Lana's eyes were suddenly drawn to the front of the restaurant as a couple came in. Her breath caught in her throat when she recognized Ron. He was paying careful attention to a tall, thin redhead with startling red lipstick on her very full lips.

Tony saw her reaction and glanced at the door. "Someone you know?" he asked.

"Just the man I've dated for over a year," Lana answered. "The man who never brought *me* to Alfonzo's."

"Then let's punish him!" Tony said, pulling his chair very close to Lana's and sliding his arm around the back of her chair. He leaned in closely and gently kissed her neck, just under her right earlobe.

"Tony!" she scolded.

"Shhh. Just follow my lead," he said, holding her gaze.

Suddenly Lana didn't have to pretend, as Tony's honey-brown eyes captivated her. She forgot about Ron until she heard his voice.

"Lana?"

"Oh, Ron. Hello," she calmly replied, glancing up at him.

"What are you doing here?" Ron asked. "And who is this?"

"I'm doing the same thing you're doing, Ron. I'm having lunch with a friend." She glanced pointedly at the redhead.

"This is Maxie," he said. "She's the new secretary at Hanzel's Corporation. We're having a business lunch so I can fill her in on office procedures."

"Hmmm. Well, this is certainly the place to do that." Lana didn't try to hide her sarcasm. "This is Anthony Angelino," she said, but didn't offer any other explanation.

Tony gave the two a slight nod of acknowledgement, then dismissed them by turning back to Lana. "So? Are you going with me to the Bahamas or not?" he asked, slightly winking at Lana.

"I'll call you tonight, Lana," Ron said, and led Maxie to their table.

"You play dirty," Lana giggled to Tony.

"I play to win," Tony said, and was about to add something when the waiter showed up with their food.

Tony didn't move his chair from its close proximity to hers. So as they ate, their arms were continually brushing against each other. If he was still trying to punish Ron, he was making a good show of it. Lana's pulse rate was on an elevated status that refused to slow down.

"Oh! Taste this. This is exquisite," Tony said, offering her his fork with a sample of food on it.

Their gaze locked and held as Lana's lips closed over the fork and pulled the food into her mouth. "That is wonderful!" she exclaimed, after savoring the food. "What is it?"

"This is Alfonzo's own version of *fegato alla veneziana*. It's made with calf's liver."

"It's delightful," Lana said. "I have to admit my knowledge of Italian food consists mostly of spaghetti, lasagna and garlic bread. I've spent most of my teen and adult life dieting, so this kind of food has basically been off limits for me."

"Well, that's just a shame. We'll have to make up for your loss, won't we?"

"Tony, you heard Jenny's concern about me getting fat for her wedding. I'm trying real hard not to gain too much weight before the wedding. But at the same time, I'm finished with starving myself. So I'd better not get too involved with experiencing all this wonderful Italian food until after the big event."

"I'd love to teach you to enjoy life, Lana. And eating is one of life's most enjoyable pleasures. Not *the* most enjoyable," he added, taking her hand and lightly kissing the back of it while giving her a wicked wink, "but one of the most."

Lana pulled her eyes from his just in time to see Ron glaring at her before leaving the restaurant.

Back at See the World, Lana made two reservations to the Bahamas for the following week for Tony. She didn't ask whom the second reservation was for, although curiosity almost got the best of her. She knew that it wasn't for her, even though he'd joked with her about going.

Later that evening, relaxing on her couch with a glass of wine, Lana smiled slightly as she wondered what it would be like to take a trip with Tony Angelino. Maybe even go on a cruise. She allowed her fantasy to progress a little before the phone interrupted her.

"Hello?" she reluctantly answered the insistent ringing.

"Lana? What were you doing fairly making out with a stranger in Alfonzo's today?" Ron's voice was strained with irritation.

"I was having lunch with Tony, like I told you, Ron. Why do you care? You told me a week ago to consider whether or not I was going to allow myself to get fat, and I haven't heard from you since. Then you show up at a place you've never hinted at taking me, with a woman that I've never seen. Now, you're questioning *me?* Ron, you need to make up your mind where you and I stand, and you need to do it quickly. If you think I'm going to wait around for you to decide if you can or can't love me just because I gain some weight, then you're sadly mistaken. I have a life ahead of me just waiting to be lived, and I'm going to live it."

"Lana, I can't believe you're willing to throw yourself away like this. Where is your pride? Don't you care about your health? Don't you care about what other people think about how you look? I'm just thinking about you."

Lana had never noticed how whiny Ron's voice sounded to her. Unlike Tony's strong, vibrant delivery. "Actually, Ron, all those things you just mentioned are not your concerns about me. They're all about how *you* feel. I'll always take care of my health, but the other things you mentioned are of no concern to me. And until they're of no concern to you, then don't call me again."

Lana carefully placed the receiver back on the base and went back to her daydreams of taking a cruise with Tony Angelino.

# Chapter 3

**"What is this, Mom?"** Lana asked, catching herself before stumbling over several pieces of luggage in the hallway as she entered her mom's house.

"For the trip with Tony," her mom said, as she leaned over and pecked a kiss on Lana's cheek, then preceded Lana to the spacious kitchen. They always referred to it as "the kitchen," but it contained a large eat-in dining room. The décor was country, and everyone gathered to the room automatically because it was so warm and welcoming. Her mom always had a hot pot of coffee made and fresh iced tea in the refrigerator.

"What?" Lana knew this was the day Tony was leaving for the Bahamas, but her mom was going with him? Was that who the second ticket was for? Her mom hadn't said a word about taking a trip. "Mom, what's going on?"

"Nothing's going on, dear. Tony's a nice guy and he needs someone to go with him to help him take some business notes. His secretary is out on pregnancy leave, you know."

"No, I didn't know, Mom. Apparently, you talk with Tony a lot more than I do."

"Well, I do have to talk with him since he's the best man at Jenny's wedding. We can't make plans without talking." Alma smiled sweetly and placed a glass of iced tea on the table in front of Lana.

"But taking a trip with him seems kind of personal. And sudden, if there's something between the two of you."

"Oh, there's definitely something between us. I really like that guy. Don't you?"

"I've only met him a couple of times, so I'm not prepared to give him two thumbs up."

"Oh, come on. You know you like him. He obviously took to you the first night you two met. I mean, he was feeding you pie! I don't think he would have done that if he hadn't liked you a little."

"He was just trying to get under Jenny's skin, Mom." Lana hoped her face didn't give away the sudden flash of memories of his lavish compliments the day they had lunch.

"What about the lunch you had with him? Did he gain any points then?"

"What do you know about that?" Had she spoken out loud again?

Alma laughed that low, sexy laugh that Lana admired so much. "Oh, I hear things. I heard that Ron didn't like all the attention you were getting from Tony."

"Again, Tony was trying to get under Ron's skin, because he was acting all persnickety about finding me with another man. And, yet, he was with another woman."

"Seems to me like Tony's always coming to your rescue," Alma mused.

"Are you jealous?"

"Not yet, baby, not yet," Alma said as she reached over and patted Lana's cheek. "I would never let a man come between you and me. Never."

"And I'd never try and take your man," Lana assured her. "I can't believe we're having this conversation. Dad's only been gone a year."

"A year can be a very long time, when you're lonely." Her mom's voice was full of sadness.

"I know, Mom. I'm sorry. I don't want you to be lonely. You deserve all the happiness you can get. I would never try to stop you from remarrying if you found someone you loved."

"Child, who said anything about getting married? I've been there and done that! I'm just talking about having a good time!"

"Mom!"

"Be a dear and see who's at the door," Alma said, standing and collecting their tea glasses and going to the sink.

Thinking that her mom was acting very strange today, Lana opened the door to find Tony Angelino looking at her.

"Is everything ready to go?"

"Oh, Tony! Come on in, but don't trip over the luggage," Alma called from the hallway.

"Hello, my favorite lady." Tony brushed past Lana and swooped Alma up into a bear hug.

Feeling totally dejected, Lana watched the two greet each other warmly, as any fantasies she may have had for Tony dissipated right before her eyes. She'd never try to take her mom's man. So much for her mom not being his type, as he'd told her at See the World.

"Are you ready to get this show on the road?" Tony asked, giving Alma a quick kiss on the cheek.

"I'm ready," Alma answered. "Just let me make a last-minute round to see if I have everything turned off and locked up. Lana, will you ride with us and say goodbye at the airport?"

"I can say goodbye now, Mom. I need to get on with my day. There's no need for me to ride to the airport with you."

"Oh, come on and go," Tony said, as Alma breezed off to make a final check of the house. "Your mom wants you to go. And I'd like that, too."

Just then Alma came back and locked the front door behind them. She grabbed Lana's arm and led her to the waiting car, not giving Lana any time to argue about going.

After the luggage was in Tony's car and he'd told the driver to take them to the airport, Lana turned to her mom and asked, "Do you want me to check the house while you're gone?" She knew the trip was booked for two weeks.

"Sure, if you have time. But don't worry about it if you're too busy."

Lana thought this was an odd statement from her mom, since she regularly stopped by her mom's house after work. It was on her way home and didn't take any time at all.

The driver stopped the car in front of the curbside check-in stand at the Mobile Regional Airport, and proceeded to set the luggage on the curb. Everyone got out of the car to say their good-byes.

Alma hugged Lana warmly and placed a lingering kiss on her cheek. "I hope you know how much I love you," she said, then turned to Tony and hugged him. "And I hope you know what you're doing," she said, and got back into the car.

The driver drove away, leaving Lana staring open-mouthed at Tony.

"Tony?"

A porter came over and started loading the luggage onto a hand truck. Tony ignored Lana's questioning look and voice as he told the porter which airline they were taking.

"We need to get in line and check in," he said, finally looking at Lana.

"I'm not going anywhere until you tell me what's going on." Her blue eyes had glazed over momentarily and were now shooting glassy shards of light at Tony.

"Now, Lana, don't be difficult. Your mom thought it would be good for you to get away for a while. She's worried that Ron will influence you negatively about your decision to stop dieting. And besides that, I don't know if she told you or not, but I need someone to take notes for me on this trip. My secretary is out on maternity leave."

"Yes, she told me. But why all the secrecy? Why didn't you just ask me to go?"

"Would you have gone?"

"No. I have a job—My job! I have to call—"

"It's all been taken care of. All you have to do is relax and enjoy a nice vacation."

By now they were at the ticket desk and the conversation stopped until the passports and tickets were stamped and the luggage tagged.

Tony handed Lana a small carry-on bag. "Your mom said you might want this," he said and winked at her. He noticed that the sparks in her eyes had settled down a little, thank goodness. He'd never seen anyone's eyes change that dramatically, that suddenly. And had never been as turned on by someone shooting him visual daggers. He was becoming consumed with Lana Clarke.

"You two really worked hard to pull this off, didn't you?" Lana remembered all the questions her mom had asked her this prior week, and understood, now, what the questions had been about. Some of the questions had been regarding the clothes that were stored at Alma's house. Alma had wondered which ones Lana could wear now that she'd gained a little weight. Lana had told her that she was up a size and would soon have to come over and pick out some clothes in that size. She was sure the luggage was full of the items she and her mom had discussed.

"Your mom did all the work," Tony said.

Lana was quiet while they hustled through the airport to get to their boarding gate. She was aware that at any time she could refuse to go on the trip. She could just turn around and walk out of the airport and go home. But since Tony and her mom had gone to so much trouble to trick her into taking this trip, the intrigue kept her feet moving along with Tony. Her first surge of anger was fading, and was being replaced by amusement at their clever scheme to send her on this trip.

But when they were finally seated and the plane was in the air, Lana turned to Tony and said, "Okay, what is this all about? Why did you and my mom go to so much trouble to practically kidnap me?"

"Your mom is worried about you, Lana. She doesn't like Ron. She thinks he's a bad influence on you. She knows you're trying to get a grip on your dieting and trying to become healthier with your eating routine, and she thinks he and Jenny might sabotage your efforts. She heard the two of them talking about you right after you made your announcement that you were going to stop dieting. They were scheming on how to get you to 'come to your senses.'"

"So my mom decides to send me on a business trip with you?"

"Actually, this isn't a business trip. When your mom was talking with me about Ron and Jenny, I suggested that I take you away for a while, so they couldn't get to you. So we came up with this idea. This is a fun trip. I've needed to take a vacation, so I thought this was a good chance to do it."

"So you took time from your life to rescue me?" Lana was finding this very hard to believe.

"Basically. But there's a factory in the Bahamas that makes a material I'm interested in, so I'll do a little business while I'm there. So see, it wasn't a totally selfless act on my part. I've been needing to get back down there, anyway. Just haven't gotten around to it."

Since she'd booked the trip, Lana knew they were landing in Nassau, the capital city of the Bahamas, but she didn't know what other arrangements Tony had made.

"This just doesn't make any sense to me. Why are you so interested in helping my mom save me from Ron and Jenny? I'm a grown woman. I can make up my mind and make my own decisions. I don't need my mom and a near stranger to protect me from my sister and boyfriend, and, it seems, from myself."

Tony leaned closer to Lana and brushed a strand of dark hair behind her ear. Then taking her chin in his large hand, he turned her face close to his and said, "Haven't you figured out that I'm very attracted to you? Your mom saw it the first night I met you at her house. She didn't say so, but I'm sure that's why she told me about Ron and Jenny. I fabricated this trip just so I could be with you. I thought if I got you away from your familiar surroundings you might be able to see that I've got it bad for you." By the time he'd ended his speech his lips were very close to Lana's, and before she could react, his lips covered hers in a kiss that shook her to her core.

He slowly pulled back from her and gazed into her dazed blue eyes. "I've wanted to do that since the first night I met you," he said. "And it was better than I'd fantasized it would be."

"You fantasized about me?" Lana's brain was still mush from

the kiss, and she felt stupid asking the question. Where had her sanity fled?

"Oh, if you only knew the thoughts I've been having about you! I can't get you off my mind, Lana. You've infected me with many impure thoughts. When you slid that piece of pie off my fork that night, I wanted to kiss you right there in front of everyone. And I've had fantasies about you ever since." His grin was mischievous as his eyes slowly perused her entire body.

Heat flowed through Lana as her body responded to his visual seduction, and that shocked her back to reality. "Tony! Surely, you didn't bring me on this trip to try and seduce me! My mom would never have endorsed something like that. She's a very old-fashioned thinker, even though she looks and acts totally modern."

"I'm not going to seduce you. But I'm gong to court you in the old-fashioned way, just like your mom would approve of. This is going to be the most romantic trip of your life, to this point. By the time we get back to Mobile you won't have any doubts as to your feelings about Ron."

"You're pretty sure of your prowess, aren't you?" Lana didn't dare tell Tony that she'd had her own fantasies about him, or the courtship might be consummated before it ever started.

"You'll find that Anthony Angelino is a very determined man. When I find something I want I'll move mountains to get it. And Lana, I haven't seen a woman that I've been attracted to since my wife died. Finding you is like being freed from a hellacious prison that I never thought I'd get out of. I still have the guilt. The guilt will always haunt me. But, along with the guilt, there's been the loneliness. Since I've met you, I feel the loneliness lifting."

"Tell me about your wife," Lana said.

"No. Not yet. In time I want to tell you everything, but not now. Not yet. Right now, I want to talk about you. About us."

"Tony, I feel compelled to remind you that I'm on my way to becoming a larger woman than I am now. Have you forgotten that? Are you going feel the same way about me then as you do now?"

His eyebrows pumped quickly up and down as he said, "Actually, my fantasies are about a larger Lana. I can't wait until then."

"You're not one of those feeder types, are you?" Lana suddenly felt uncomfortable with that thought.

"What's a feeder?" he asked, slightly leaning back from her.

"It's someone, usually a man, who gets his kicks by feeding his woman until she's really big."

She didn't expect the laugh that escaped from him. "What I have in mind for you would actually be referred to as wining and dining, I believe. I just want to see you healthy and happy. And, I have to admit, I do like a woman with well-rounded curves. If that makes me weird, then so be it. But I'd rather think it's just my preference."

Could this really be happening? Lana wondered. She was tempted to pinch herself to see if she was dreaming. But if this was a dream, she hoped she'd never wake up, she decided, as Tony took her hand and kissed the back of it before placing the two joined hands in his lap.

Where did she want this to lead? Was she ready to actually get involved with someone? Was that what Tony wanted, or was he just playing with her emotions? He seemed very sincere, which lead to another question—why? Why her?

She'd never really believed that her relationship with Ron would go anywhere. They'd never had sex. Ron made advances, but she'd always found a way to deter him, which was easy because Ron wasn't a pushy person. And she doubted he'd be an ardent lover. Ron was just kind of dispassionate.

Tony's thumb, making slow circular motions on the top of her hand, brought her out of her reverie. She became almost mesmerized watching his thumb and feeling the emotions the soft touch sent chorusing through her.

"What's on your mind?" he asked. His voice was low and seductive. It was obvious he knew exactly what he was doing to her. Her entire body felt warm and languid. His brown eyes captured and held hers, their depths unfathomable to the point that she feared she might sink and drown in them.

"I think I'm going to like this wining and dining and courting thing," she whispered huskily.

# Chapter 4

**Lana stood on the balcony and gazed out** over the huge expanse of ocean view. She'd expected to be taken to a hotel when they arrived at Nassau. Instead they'd been picked up in a private car and brought to this beautiful oceanfront home. Anthony Angelino's home.

Reality had hit Lana with a jolt. She knew nothing about Tony Angelino, and yet here she was alone with him in his home. *One* of his homes, it seemed.

The house was a sand-colored wooden construction with long steps leading from the beach to a porch that encircled it. Patio furniture, wooden rockers, two swings, and miscellaneous potted plants created a welcoming atmosphere everywhere one looked on the porch. Doors from all four sides of the lower level of the house opened onto the porch. Inside the ceilings were high, with ceiling fans whirling, causing sun-filtered shadows to flit across the hardwood floors. The entire lower level of the house was open, making it possible for anyone working in the kitchen to communicate with someone sitting in the living area. The four bedrooms were upstairs. Each bedroom had its own private bath and balcony.

Lana was standing on the balcony of the bedroom that she'd been shown to when they arrived. From where she stood she could see a large dock and boathouse with a boat in it. She assumed the dock and boat were also Tony's.

Turning to go back inside to unpack her suitcases, she wondered how much longer Tony would be on the phone call he'd gotten as soon as they'd arrived. And she walked right into him.

"Enjoying the view?" he asked, as his arms closed around her to help steady them. "Hmm. This feels perfect!" he said, pulling her closer. "We fit together like two puzzle pieces."

"Tony!" Lana tried to protest, but he was right. Being in his arms felt perfect. As if she'd come home. And his probing kiss melted her protests for the time being.

"Beautiful Lana," he said, looking down at her kiss-swollen lips, then rained kisses over her entire face. "Do you know how crazy you make me?"

Lana was finding it hard to get enough air in her lungs to answer him, but it didn't matter because he'd again captured her lips in his. Their breathing became one. He breathed in her expelled breath and she, in turn, breathed in his. It was one of the most erotic things she'd ever experienced.

Emotions charged through her. Emotions she'd never experienced with anyone. She knew she was losing control. She reluctantly pushed Tony away just enough to talk. "Tony," she managed weakly, "Please. We have to slow down."

He was obviously as affected as she was. He looked at her through half-closed eyes and smiled. "You're right," he said huskily. "But this slow courtship is going to be a lot harder than I'd imagined."

**The next few days were a whirlwind** of activity. Tony took her to the best restaurants, where he ordered the most expensive wines and treated her to exquisite Bahamian foods. Lana didn't usually care for seafood, but found she loved the Bahamian style of preparing it.

One of the many sites they toured was the Queen's Staircase, a flight of sixty-six steps linking Fort Fincastle to Princess Margaret Hospital. Tony explained that the staircase was probably the most famous architectural sight in Nassau. Lana was intrigued that the staircase was not built in the typical sense, but that slaves had hand-carved the stairs out of coral-based sandstone at the end of the 18th century.

They snorkeled, they went deep-sea fishing, and they strolled along the beautiful beaches. Lana loved the horse-drawn surrey ride through the downtown district with its colorful local shops, fascinating examples of colonial architecture, museums, culture and history.

Through it all, Tony kept his word to court her slowly. He treated her like a queen. He was ever attentive. Touching her, holding her hand, drooping an arm around her shoulders or waist and stealing kisses when she least expected it. But he never took his advances any further than an occasional very steamy, tantalizing kiss.

Lana's favorite times were when they just sat on the porch at Tony's house, like they were doing now, enjoying the sunset over the quiet water.

She'd never felt as much at home with a man as she did with Tony. Yet she'd never had a man excite her as much, either. She was beginning to wish he'd forget about taking things slow and easy. Just looking at him and the promise in his eyes kept her turned on to the point of distraction. She felt like screaming "take me!"

The thought brought a smile to her lips, and Tony asked, "Share the joke?"

Not realizing he'd been watching her, Lana's face turned red at the thought of telling him what she'd been thinking. "I was just enjoying this beautiful view," she lied.

"Hmm. Wonder why that would bring such a becoming blush to your face," he said. "I think you're lying to me. I think you were having naughty thoughts about us," he surmised, as if reading her mind.

"I was not!"

"Were, too."

"Why would you think that?" She wondered if she'd actually moaned out loud, or in some way given him a clue to her thoughts.

"Because you're probably the most sensual woman I've ever known. I think you think about us a lot."

"Well, how could I not? You're always touching me or kissing me. You keep me constantly aroused, and you're doing it on purpose!" Oh no! She hadn't meant to just spit it out, like that!

"See. That's what I mean. How many women would admit that they were turned on, so openly? I love that about you. Your honesty is refreshing." He moved from the chair he'd been sitting in to join her in the swing. "Mary was so different from you. She was shy and inhibited when it came to sex and saying what was on her mind."

"Mary was your wife?"

"Yes. But that's another story for another time," he said, and rested his arm on the back of the swing behind her shoulders.

"When?" Lana asked.

"I don't know, Lana. When it feels right. But right now it doesn't feel right. Right now I have other things on my mind besides talking about the past. I have the present on my mind. You are the only thing I want to think about." And he pulled her to him in a warm, gentle kiss.

"So I keep you turned on, huh?" he asked, pulling slightly away and looking down at her. "Prove it. Let me feel how turned on you are," he said, as his hand slid slowly into the waistband of her slacks.

But the persistent ringing of his cell phone demanded that he abandon his mission and answer it.

"Hello!" His answer was less than cordial. "Right now? Can't it wait?" Irritation resounded in his voice. "Okay," he finally agreed.

After signing off the phone he said, "I have to go inside and do a conference call with a couple of my store managers. There's been a tiff and one of them is threatening to call the police on the other one. So I'd better see if I can calm them down. But I'll be back out here as soon as I can, and we'll continue where we left off." His grin told Lana that he was feeling very wicked tonight.

Panicking, suddenly afraid that what she'd wished for was about to happen, Lana decided to take a stroll along the beach while he made his call. She had to think about what might happen. Was she ready for a serious relationship with Anthony Angelino? Or had she just been enjoying all the attention she'd been getting?

Holding her shoes in her hands, Lana strolled along the sandy beach. The soft, balmy breeze rustled her dark hair as the water gently lapped at her bare feet. Her thoughts were in turmoil when she tried to reason her way around how quickly she was becoming emotionally involved with Tony.

She considered herself an intelligent woman. One who kept close guard on herself when it came to men. She never wanted to be one of those vulnerable women who fell for the first line that came her way. And for that reason, she'd become just a little skeptical when it came to dealing with guys. That's one reason she'd allowed herself to stay involved with Ron all these months. Ron wasn't an assertive man. He was safe. Didn't demand anything from her. In fact, she'd wondered sometimes if he were even interested in sex. Or if maybe she just didn't turn him on. But he was comfortable. Someone to go out with on the weekends. Someone she could depend on.

But after being around Tony, comfort wasn't enough. She realized that her life had become stale and boring. And now that she had some excitement going on, she recognized how much she'd missed it. But not just anybody's excitement. Tony had reminded her that she was missing the literal thrill of living. The exhilaration. The anticipation of getting up every morning. The enthusiasm of little things that happened during the day.

The hand on Lana's arm interrupted her thoughts. Expecting to find Tony beside her, she looked around into the most menacing face she'd ever encountered. Snatching her arm from the man's grip, she opened her mouth to scream, and he laid the cold metal of a pistol against her throat.

Lana stared into bloodshot, unnaturally light-blue eyes. An aura of evil surrounded the man. He wasn't tall, maybe an inch taller than her five foot, six inch frame, with greasy black hair.

"Make one sound and you'll be shark bait," he warned through tobacco-stained teeth. His breath reeked of beer and garlic. "You know that pretty sister of yours that's about to get married? And that sexy mama of yours that's just waiting for some man to relieve her tensions? If you want them to live, you'd best just walk quietly along with me and not make a scene. Otherwise, they'll die a horrible death."

As he talked, he led Lana toward the boathouse that she had admired from her balcony. She glanced expectantly at the house, hoping Tony had come back outside to the porch and was looking for her.

"Don't worry, darlin', he'll be tied up for a long time with those two arguing store managers. I made sure their misunderstanding was a good one." They were at the boathouse now, and he shoved Lana through the door into the shadows. The fading light gave just enough visibility for Lana to see a rowboat gently rocking in the water beside the larger motorboats.

"Yeah, I can see why Tony fell for you. You're quite a looker," her captor said, reaching out and placing a hand on one of her breasts.

Lana slapped his hand away and stepped back from him. "You touch me one more time, and you'll be the one the sharks will taste," she ground through clenched teeth. Now that they were out of sight from Tony the man had seemed to relax a little, and she could probably get away with being a little aggressive. A lot aggressive, when she found the chance. He was letting the gun dangle by his side.

His laugh was nasty as he pushed her toward the waiting rowboat. "Get in the boat, bitch. If I hadn't already made plans, I'd sample your feisty wares before I turn you over to the sharks. But I have a schedule to keep, so let's get going."

Darkness settled in as he maneuvered the boat out of the boathouse into the open water. Lana thought she heard Tony shouting her name from somewhere in the distance. The man heard it too, because he poked the gun in her ribs and warned, "Don't even think about answering him."

Lightning flashed across the sky in the distance, and Lana realized the water had become restless. For the first time she felt fear. Up until now she'd fully expected to be able to get away from this lunatic, or that Tony would come looking for her. But now she realized she was in real danger.

"What is your name? Why are you doing this to me?" she asked, trying to keep the panic from her voice.

"Yeah, like I'm going to give you any information," the man jeered. "You think I'm stupid or something?"

"Actually, yes. I do think you're stupid to think you can get away with this, but you must not be too sure of your plans if you're afraid to tell me about them. Maybe you're afraid that your plan won't work. That I'll get back to shore. Otherwise you wouldn't be a coward about telling me what this is all about. Surely if I'm going to die I have the right to know why."

"You have no rights!" he screamed. Then realizing what he'd done, he lowered his voice and said, "You think you're really smart, don't you? You can't yell, but you think you can make me give myself away. Good try, but it won't work. We're too far out now. Tony boy can't hear anything."

"But you're still afraid to tell me why you want to kill me. I've never done anything to you."

"Lady, I ain't afraid of nothing! And if you were smart, you'd stop taunting me."

"Why? Aren't you going to kill me anyway? What do I have to fear? It seems my fate is sealed in your mind. Too bad you don't trust your plan enough to talk to me."

He was rowing directly into the storm, which was coming closer by the moment. "You know what, just to prove to you how confident I am, I'll tell you why I'm doing this. Hell, I'll even tell you my name. My name is Dan. Dan Smith. I went to college with Tony. Once upon a time we were friends. Then he stole my girl. Stole her right from under my nose. I made a pact with the devil right then that Anthony Angelino would never find happiness. He'd never be with the woman he loved. I've made sure of that all along. And I'll continue to make sure of that."

"So I have to die because you don't want Tony to be with me?"

"You learn fast, bitch." His look and laugh were, indeed, diabolical as a flash of lightning illuminated his distorted face.

It was hard for Lana to believe that the person before her had been to college. But it was even harder to believe that Tony had been his friend. Maybe he was lying. Maybe he didn't even know Tony.

"Ah, yes, good old Tom. Right on time," Dan said, bringing Lana's attention to approaching lights from an oncoming boat. The motorboat pulled up beside their rowboat and stopped.

Tom, a huge black man, reached over the side of the motorboat and helped pull Dan in beside him, leaving Lana in the rowboat alone.

"Poor Lana," Dan said, "She made the mistake of rowing too far out and got caught in this bad storm that's upon us. She lost an oar and couldn't get back to shore." He laughed his crazy laugh as a flash of lightning gave enough light for Lana to see him hurl the oar as far into the distance as he could.

Only then did she realize he'd taken one of the oars with him, leaving her with just one. There's no way she could row with just one oar. She'd never rowed a boat with two, so she knew she'd wind up going around in circles with one oar.

"Boss, you didn't tell me what this was all about when you asked me to meet you here," Tom said. Lana heard the disapproval in his voice.

Dan heard it too. Tom should never have disapproved of Dan. Or was Dan just following the rest of his plan? "Stand up, Tom," he ordered.

"Why, Boss?"

"Just stand up, dammit! Don't argue with me!"

Tom stood up and Dan shot him at point blank range, knocking him over the side of the boat. He barely missed landing in the rowboat with Lana, which would probably have capsized it, if he had.

In horror, she watched the water settle around the big man, then watched Dan Smith toss the pistol into the water and roar away, leaving nothing but the pending storm and churning waves.

# Chapter 5

**Fat drops of rain splattered here and there** around Lana as the wind picked up and rocked the small rowboat. Clutching each side of the boat, she gazed helplessly around. In the flashing lightning, she could see the waves getting larger.

Was she going to die? Was this really the end of her life? NO! She would *not* allow those thoughts to panic her. She had to come up with a survival plan. But as a wave carried the boat up about six feet and swooshed it back down, just holding on was the only survival plan that came to mind at the moment.

As the boat settled down a little, Lana was aware of a thumping at the side of the boat. Ready to scream at some sea monster, she was exhilarated to see the second oar floating alongside the boat. She quickly grabbed it and hauled it in beside her.

Just having the oar back gave Lana new hope. She knew rowing wouldn't do her any good in a storm like the one pounding down on her. But if she lived through the storm, maybe she would be able to row to some shore and find her way back to Tony. Suddenly things didn't seem so hopeless.

The lightning was continuous now, zigzagging around her like Fourth of July fireworks gone bad. And the thunder was deafening. Lana's greatest urge was to lie down in the boat, cover her ears with her hands and squeeze her eyes closed as tightly as possible. In fact, she reasoned, that might not be a bad idea. Might be better than sitting up straight just inviting the lightning to strike her.

She was about to change positions when she caught a glimpse of something bobbing in the water just ahead of the boat. Reaching for an oar, she got ready to strike the object if it turned out to be a shark or some unknown sea creature. But as the boat churned closer to the bobbing object, she saw what appeared to be arms moving in the water.

Someone was swimming! Toward her! But it was so dark she couldn't tell who or what it was, even with the lightning. A sheet of rain peppered her face, blinding her even further.

"Lana!" She heard the voice calling her name as she frantically tried to wipe the rain from her eyes. But who was calling her name? This was crazy! Who could be swimming in the ocean in this storm, calling her name? Was it the angel of death coming after her?

She was too frightened to scream as she felt the side of the boat swoop down and watched the huge figure hurl itself into the boat in front of and partially on top of her.

"I'm sorry. I hope I didn't hurt you," the figure said as it up-righted itself and sat to face her.

"Tom?"

"I think so," he answered, coughing and wiping the water from his face.

"But how? I watched Dan shoot you pointblank in the chest. I thought I'd watched a man die. How are you alive?"

"Ah, the wonders of bulletproof vests. Look, I'll explain everything to you, but right now we need to see if we can ride this storm out. Is that an oar you're holding? At least we have one. I know Dan took the other one with him onto the boat." He reached over and took the oar from her hand.

"Actually, he threw that oar into the water after he shot you. But it caught up with me a few minutes ago. We have two oars again."

"That's great news!" Tom said. He reached for the second oar and started maneuvering the boat to try and keep it upright as the wind and waves picked up.

Lana looked at the man who sat across from her. He had been

in on the plan to kill her. Yet Dan had shot him. And did he say "bulletproof vest?" Was he friend or foe? Did he plan to finish her off?

Nothing Tom had said made her feel threatened. And he was doing his best to keep the boat afloat in the storm. If he wanted to kill her, all he had to do was toss her overboard and it would be easier for him to maneuver the boat.

She started to gain a little hope. If she lived through this storm, maybe Tom would help her get back to Tony.

"If you will, sit down in the bottom of the boat so we won't be so top heavy," Tom shouted to Lana through the rain and wind. "I know it will be uncomfortable, but it will help balance the boat a little."

Lana wiggled to a cramped sitting position in the center bottom of the boat, facing Tom. He constantly monitored the swirling waves around them, and tried to use the oars to maneuver the small boat to keep it upright. His battle seemed to go on forever, but finally Lana realized the lightning and thunder were becoming less frequent and the wind seemed to be settling down a little. But the rain still came in torrents, soaking them to the skin.

After what seemed like hours, and several near capsizes, the waves started to subside to a gentle roll. Tom placed both oars beside him in the boat and slumped with his head lowered to his chest, heaving great breaths of air. Lana knew he must be exhausted, so she didn't try to make conversation. She'd wait until he was rested, then she'd ask him the questions that crashed around in her mind.

Gradually the storm moved away from them. The rain stopped and the boat rocked gently like a cradle soothing a baby to sleep. With the lightning gone, the night was pitch black. Where was the moon when you needed it?

Tom's voice penetrated the darkness. "Since I don't have any idea where we are, it wouldn't be wise for me to try and row anywhere. We might wind up farther out to sea than we already are. It's best to just sit here and wait for daylight."

"Who are you?" Lana asked. "You drove a boat to meet a man

who was trying to kill me. You got shot. And now you've saved me. Are you going to kill me later? If so, why didn't you just dump me overboard during the storm?"

"Whoa! Calm down, Lana. You don't want hysteria setting in now that the crisis is over."

"Is it over? Am I safe? I need to know," Lana said.

"You're safe. Very safe. My name is Tom Hoover. I'm a private investigator Tony hired after his wife died. I'm retired from the Mobile police force."

"Why did Tony hire a private detective after his wife died? Did he expect foul play?"

"So he hasn't told you about his suspicions?"

"He keeps saying he'll tell me about her sometime, but he hasn't yet."

"Well, maybe I'm speaking out of turn, but I feel like you need to know the facts. Obviously you're in danger, since Dan Smith tried to kill you.

"Dan and Tony were friends in college. Dan was crazy about a college girl named Mary Manelli. Mary wasn't that interested in Dan. But Dan couldn't accept the fact that Mary didn't want him. He'd become obsessed with her.

"As it turned out, Mary perceived herself to be really in love with Tony, but Tony wouldn't pursue her because he knew how crazy Dan was about her. After they got out of college Dan took a job in another town, so Tony and Mary had a chance to get together. It didn't take long for them to fall in love and get married.

"Not long after their wedding Dan showed back up, accusing Tony of stealing 'his girl.' He said he'd gone away to build a fortune that would be worthy of Mary. He claimed he'd asked her to wait for him so they could get married.

"Mary declared she didn't remember any of that, but it didn't matter because she'd never loved him. They finally had to have a restraining order put on Dan to keep him away from them.

"After some time passed, Tony and Mary's son was born and everything seemed to have settled down. Dan seemed to have dropped out of the picture.

"Tony was out of town on a business trip when he got the news that his house had burned down and Mary and the baby were dead. He was devastated. Went through a couple of years of pure hell. His family and friends wondered if he'd ever get over it.

"But Tony had questions surrounding the fire. Mary was an avid non-smoker. Tony said she'd almost embarrass him on occasions when someone would light up around her and the baby. But according to the reports, the fire had started because she'd been smoking in bed. A clump of melted cigarette filters, the remains of a pack of cigarettes, was found in the ashes where the nightstand would have been. Tony refuses to believe that Mary had taken up smoking.

"And the other suspicious thing was that Dan's college ring was found in Mary's car. Almost as if Dan was sending a message that he and Mary had been seeing each other. Of course that's only speculation."

"So Tony thinks Dan killed Mary and the baby?" Lana was horrified at the thought.

"There's only the circumstantial evidence until now. Tony has had me following Dan for several years, and although he's a weird person, I've never found anything of substance until this attempt on you."

"How did you get involved with him to come after me?"

"I knew Tony had planned to come to the Bahamas. When I realized that Dan had plans to come here, too, I got really suspicious. I wondered if he had foul play on his mind. So I followed him here and hung real close to him. I 'accidentally' overheard him asking if anyone would be interested in driving a motorboat to pick him up after a secret rendezvous. I volunteered, and he explained that he was going to meet a woman, but she was married so they had to meet on an island for their rendezvous. And when it was over, I was to meet them and take him back to shore so she could go home alone. I was pretty sure this had something to do with you, but didn't know he actually meant to leave you stranded until he took the oar into the boat with us."

As he talked, the darkness around them began to fade to a gray haze. Lana had never experienced the approach of dawn while sitting in a rowboat surrounded by an ocean. An ocean that was, thankfully, very serene.

The gradual light revealed the man before her. She hadn't had a chance to really look at him during the storm. She stuck with her first impression that he was huge. His wet clothes clung to his muscled frame and she could tell he was in excellent shape. That was probably why he was able to keep them upright during the storm.

She saw him slightly wince when he shifted his position on the seat.

"Are you hurt?" she asked. After all, he'd been shot and then had to chase her boat down and crawl into it.

"I'm okay. Just beginning to get sore from taking a bullet at close range like that. Bulletproof vests might save your life, but they don't always protect from the impact of the bullet, if it's up close and personal."

"So where do we go from here?" Lana asked. "Tony hasn't told me any of the story you just shared with me, so do I tell him that I know?"

"Yes. Be honest with him. And I'll tell him everything that's happened tonight. He needs to know that you're in danger so he'll be more careful with you."

"Well, Tony and I aren't exactly an item, so he can't be with me all the time. I'll just have to watch my back for myself."

"I have a feeling you'll be seeing a lot more of Tony than you realize. Since Mary's death, he hasn't shown any interest in a woman until you came along. How do you feel about him? You aren't just playing him because he has money, are you?"

The question surprised and rankled Lana. Who was this man to question her intentions?

Apparently he saw the anger flash in her blue eyes. "Tony saved my life once. That's all you need to know about that, but I don't want to see him hurt. He's a good man to have on your side. In fact, he's the best man you could have on your side. Be honest with him about your feelings and intentions. Don't hurt him."

Lana was about to retort when she heard the distant sound of an approaching boat. Tom heard it too.

"That's the Coast Guard. I'm sure Tony's been up all night looking for you. When we get back to the station, I'm going to disappear as soon as I can. I don't know when you'll see me again, but I'll be keeping an eye on you. If you see me in public, don't acknowledge me. I don't want anyone to know that we're acquainted. And I want Dan Smith to think I died last night.

"I can't say it was a pleasure spending the night with you, but under different circumstances, I'm sure it would be a pleasure to be with you." For the first time, he smiled. The smile lit his entire face. And suddenly Lana felt safer just knowing that he'd be keeping an eye out for her, as he promised.

"I can see why Tony has fallen for you. You're a brave woman. You didn't whine once last night. Plus, you're beautiful. I can see Tony being very happy with you."

"Whoa, we aren't married yet," Lana protested. But the huge Coast Guard boat pulling up beside them made it impossible for Tom to hear her.

**A whirlwind of activity followed their rescue,** and Lana didn't see Tom again. She realized too late that she hadn't thanked him for saving her life. She'd make sure that Tony relayed her gratitude.

Once at the Coast Guard station and finished with the questions she was asked, Lana waited impatiently for Tony to get there. Her clothes were still wet and the air conditioning was cold. She sat huddled in a chair, reliving the night before.

Reality was creeping in, now that the drama was over. Her life was in danger because she was associated with Tony Angelino. She should be fish bait this morning. That's what Dan Smith had planned. A shiver shook her entire body.

"Ma'am, would you like this blanket to wrap around you?" A kind-looking officer handed her a soft blanket, and Lana quickly wrapped it around herself.

"Thank you," she said between chattering teeth.

"I think your nerves are taking over, now that you're safe. Mr.

Angelino will be here soon to get you. Would you like a cup of coffee?"

"No, I'm fine," Lana said. She didn't think she could hold a coffee cup because of her shaking hands. If Tom could see her now, he wouldn't think she was so brave.

As the warmth from the blanket soaked into Lana, she began to relax. Her teeth stopped clacking together and her hands stopped shaking. She rested her head on the back of the chair and was about to doze when she heard the door open. Looking up, she saw Tony rushing toward her.

"Sir, we need to talk with you first." An officer stopped Tony before he got to Lana.

But Tony pulled away from him and came to her. "Are you okay? What happened? Where did you go? I've been crazy all night, looking for you."

"Sir, we can answer your questions if you'll give us a little time," the officer persisted.

"I'm okay, Tony. I'll explain everything later. Just see what they want so we can get out of here," she said.

Lana watched Tony being led into an office and the door close behind him. Had Tom told the Coast Guard everything? She rested her head against the chair again, and was soon asleep.

A hand in her hair and lips on hers brought Lana out of the deep sleep she'd fallen into. "Come on, baby, let's go home." Tony's concerned look brought Lana fully awake. How could a voice be so gentle while a face looked ready to kill?

She stood and handed the damp blanket to the waiting officer. Tony led her from the station to his car. "I'm taking you home and feeding you a big breakfast. Then you're going to take a warm shower and sleep for as long as you want to. Then I want to hear everything from the moment I last saw you on the porch yesterday."

"I can tell you now," Lana volunteered.

"No. You're too tired. I'm afraid you'll forget something. I'll call Tom while you sleep and get his side of the story. Although he told the officers most of it, I'm sure he left off some key factors for the sake of safety."

"I didn't have a chance to thank him for saving my life. But how do you thank a person for something that huge?"

"Trust me, Lana. I'll thank him for both of us."

When they reached Tony's house, it seemed his plans had changed a little. He instructed his housekeeper, Ally, to fix eggs, toast and bacon and bring it to the bathroom as soon as it was done.

Lana stood tiredly and listened to him issue instructions. "Come with me," he said to Lana, and took her arm and steered her upstairs. When they got to her room, he proceeded to undress her.

"What are you doing?" she screeched, grabbing his hands to stop the motion of her shirt being pulled over her head. But it was too late. Her wet shirt lay crumpled in a damp heap on the floor.

"Even more beautiful than I'd imagined," he whispered, gazing at her heaving breasts. Her damp bra didn't leave much to the imagination. Reaching around her, he deftly unhooked her bra and let it slide to the floor with her shirt. A low moan escaped from his throat as he gently cupped and kissed each breast in turn.

By now Lana had forgotten how tired she was. She'd forgotten how wonderful a bath sounded. She'd forgotten everything except the man before her. She stood tongue-tied and immobilized as he continued to slide her pants down her hips and help her step out of them. But she gasped as he slid her panties down and kissed their path to the floor.

Disappointment flooded her as he stood and left her and went to the bathroom. She heard water running in the tub, and soon he was back. He led her to the waiting tub, which was filling with water and bubbles. Holding her hand while she stepped in, he guided her down and watched as the bubbles slowly rose and covered the parts he coveted the most.

Lana's entire body throbbed and hummed. She'd never experienced anything as sensual as this. Had never wanted anything as much as she wanted Tony to make love to her, right now.

A gentle knock on the door announced the arriving breakfast. Tony took the food and pulled a vanity stool over and sat down in front of the tub. No words were spoken as he slowly fed Lana the food that filled the plate, while she luxuriated in warm bubbles that covered everything except her head.

Food was the last thing on her mind, but Lana realized how hungry she was when she took the first bite. She would have stopped eating immediately if Tony had offered to take her to bed. But he didn't. He slowly fed her, and devoured her with his eyes while she ate. After the food was gone, he set the plate aside and picked up a sponge and started to bathe her.

"Tony!" Lana's voice was weak, but she protested anyway.

"Shhhh. Just relax, my love. Just relax and enjoy being safe."

*How can I relax when you're driving me crazy?* Lana's brain screamed. Tony left the sponge floating in the water and proceeded to bathe her with his naked hands. Holding each arm up and massaging it slowly down to the armpit, then surrounding each breast, cupping, molding, kneading it while it floated in the water, before moving on down to her most private section.

At her moan, he whispered, "Tell me what you want, Lana. Tell me. Is it this?" he asked, gently pressing where she ached the most.

"Yes! Oh, yes!" she moaned, and gave in to the release that racked her body with wave after wave of ecstasy.

"Now you can sleep, *cara mia*—my darling. Now you can sleep without any haunting dreams."

Tony dried her off and led her to the bed. She hoped he'd get in bed with her, but he tucked the covers around her, softly kissed her on the lips, then left her to sleep.

# *Chapter 6*

**Lana drifted slowly, reluctantly** from the dream she was having. She was a child again, lying in the grass, looking up at the blue sky and making figures from cloud formations. The sun was shining warmly on her and she felt good.

As her eyes finally opened, she realized the setting sun was beaming into the open window and her bed was flooded in sunlight. Looking at the clock, she saw that it was four P.M. She'd slept most of the day!

Sitting up in bed, she wondered where Tony was. Tony. Then she remembered the bath and smiled. *Tony.* Then she remembered more about the bath and blushed. *Tony!*

She'd been so exhausted from the night before, she'd let him treat her as if she was incapable of taking care of herself. Every part of her independent self recoiled at being a wilting flower. Yet it had felt good to allow Tony to take care of her. And he'd done a splendid job. Again, she smiled.

Oh, well. She'd have to be more careful and not let him turn her into some needy, clinging vine. Hopefully that wasn't the kind of woman he wanted, because that sure wasn't the kind she was.

She pulled on a pair of jeans and realized the snap was a little snug. All this wining and dining was starting to put the pounds on. Would Jenny notice when she got home? Of course she would. Jenny *always* noticed when someone gained weight. Always noticed and commented.

*Too bad*, Lana thought, and headed for the kitchen to find some food. It had been a long time since Tony had fed her breakfast.

She looked in all the places downstairs where Tony usually hung out, but he wasn't around. His SUV wasn't outside, so he was gone.

Suddenly feeling alone and vulnerable, Lana was about to check the doors to see if they were locked when Ally, the housekeeper, came in from a side door.

"Did you get your nap out?" Ally asked. She was probably in her mid-thirties, tall and slim with slightly graying hair.

Lana got the feeling that Ally didn't care much for her. She wondered why. "Yes. I can't believe that I slept that long."

"Well, when a person stays out all night and parties, they usually sleep all day."

*Party?* Ally thought Lana had been out all night partying? Is that what Tony had told her? Maybe he wanted what happened to be kept a secret. Lana decided not to contradict her. Instead she asked, "Is it okay if I fix a sandwich?"

"You want me to fix you one?" Ally asked reluctantly.

"No. I'm very capable of making my own sandwich, but thank you, anyway."

She was aware of Ally watching her as she went into the kitchen.

Lana made a sandwich of smoked turkey, mustard and lettuce on whole wheat bread, got a bottle of water and was about to head for the porch when she remembered Dan Smith. Feeling too vulnerable to be outside by herself, she sat down at the dining room table instead.

"Nobody's ever been here, except Tony, who was willing to wait on themselves," Ally volunteered, standing at the opposite end of the table. "Sorry if I was rude to you."

So that was it. Ally didn't dislike Lana, she just didn't like being taken advantage of, and she assumed Lana was going to demand a lot from her. She should have known better. Lana and Tony had been in the house for over a week, and Lana had never asked

Ally to do anything.

"Does Tony bring a lot of folks here?" she asked.

"Not anymore. He used to when his wife was alive. I didn't like her friends. I didn't like her much, either."

"Why?" Lana asked, motioning for Ally to sit down. It was obvious Ally wanted to talk, so maybe Lana needed to listen. Listening to Tony's housekeeper wasn't exactly gossip, was it? After all, if she was going to get involved with Tony, she needed to know as much as she could about him and his past.

"Let's just say she made me earn my keep when she came around," Ally said. "She could be a real pain in the butt. I never understood why Tony fell for her."

Lana saw a flash of something in Ally's eyes that made her uncomfortable. This probably wasn't such a good idea, she realized. Maybe Ally was in love with Tony herself. Maybe she resented any woman that he brought here.

"How long have you known Tony?" Lana asked.

"Since we were in college. But he doesn't even remember me. I was in his art class, but I dropped out the first semester. When I saw his ad in the paper for a housekeeper in the Bahamas, I applied. I figured this would be a fairly easy way for me to earn a living and feel like I was on vacation at the same time. Odd how life slaps some people in the face, while it pats others on top of their little heads and gives them everything their hearts desire." Bitterness crept in, and her voice became hard.

This woman had a story, and Lana needed to know what it was. But she didn't want to seem too curious. If Ally knew Tony in college, did she know Dan Smith? Could she ask without seeming obvious?

"Did you know Tony very well in college?"

"I knew him, but he didn't know me. He was too busy trying to snatch Mary away from Dan."

"Dan?" *This was too easy*, Lana thought.

But Ally realized she'd said too much. "I'd better start dinner. Tony said he wanted to eat in tonight." And she abruptly left the table.

Hmm. Very interesting. Lana took her plate back to the kitchen and put it in the dishwasher before taking her water and heading for the porch. Maybe Tony would be back soon.

"Thanks," Ally mumbled as Lana left the kitchen. Lana assumed the thanks was for putting her plate in the dishwasher.

Several sailboats dotted the horizon as Lana relaxed on the porch and looked out over the ocean. The peaceful scene before her made a lie of the horrors she'd been through the night before in those same waters. Waters that had come so close to being her grave. A shiver of remembered fear and pending danger dampened the beauty before her.

Would Dan Smith try to kill her again when he found out she was alive? After hearing Tom's story, she was convinced he would. Had Dan killed Mary? If so, how did he make it look like an accident?

Restless from the questions that swirled through her head, Lana got up and strolled along the porch that wrapped around the house. The floors were painted white and waxed to a high shine. Her soft-soled sneakers made no noise as she passed from one flowing potted plant to the next. The plants were exotic. Some were scented, others weren't, but they were all equally beautiful. Just touching their soft velvety petals and breathing in their fragrance brought peace to Lana's jangled nerves.

She was about to go back to the front of the house when she heard Ally's voice. Ally was seated behind a large plant and wasn't aware of Lana's approach.

"She's not dead," Lana heard her hushed voice say. Silence. "No, the Coast Guard rescued her this morning. That's all I know." Silence. "No, I tried to get Tony to talk to me, but he was closed-mouthed."

Lana could tell the conversation was winding down, so she turned and hurried back the way she'd come. She'd just sat back down in a rocker when Tony's black SUV pulled up. He jumped from the vehicle and hurried to her. She stood up to greet him.

He wrapped her in a bear hug and held her for several seconds. "Did you get any rest?" he asked.

"I slept all day!" Lana said. "I haven't been up that long, actually."

"We have a lot of talking to do. I want to hear everything that happened. I've asked Ally to fix dinner here tonight so we can have a relaxed meal and conversation." He stopped talking and gazed down at Lana. "You have no idea what hell I went through last night. I was afraid I'd lost you, too." His voice cracked as he pulled Lana close again and captured her lips with his.

This wasn't a seductive or playful kiss, like the ones she was used to. This kiss claimed her. Branded her as his. The depths of this kiss shook Lana to her core.

Reluctantly he ended the kiss and led Lana to the swing where they'd been sitting the night before. Pulling her down beside him, he wrapped his arm around her shoulders and drew her close to him.

"I want us to leave in the morning. I want to go back to Mobile. I have a lot of things to take care of, and I think you'll be safer there around friends and family. I hate to cut our vacation short, but under the circumstances, I think it's best.

"I'd wanted to check out a factory that makes batik fabric, and wanted to take you with me, but I went ahead today and checked them out and talked with the sales manager about ordering some of their garments for my stores. This way we can leave in the morning. Is that okay with you?"

"Whatever you think is best. I'm not afraid to stay here, but I won't be wandering off by myself anymore, that's for sure," Lana declared.

"After we eat, I want to hear everything," he said.

"I don't think that's a good idea, Tony," Lana said, afraid that the walls had ears.

"Why?"

"Let's take a walk on the beach," she said.

Puzzled, Tony stood and followed Lana down the steps. When they reached the water's edge and Lana was convinced that no listening ears could overhear them, she said, "How much do you know about Ally?"

"She's been with me for five years. She's never given me any problems. Always did what I asked her—why do you ask that?"

"She says she knew you and Dan in college."

"What?"

"She said she was in your art class, but you never noticed her. And that you didn't remember her when she came to work for you. Tony, I think she's in love with you. And I don't think she likes me very much. And I know she didn't like Mary."

"Wait. Wait. How do you know all this?"

"We had a long conversation this afternoon."

"Did she say anything else?"

"She said you never noticed her because you were too busy trying to snatch Mary away from Dan. When I indicated that I wanted to know who Dan was, she immediately stopped the conversation and went to start dinner."

"She said I was trying to snatch Mary away from Dan? That's not true! Mary was chasing me the entire time Dan was chasing her! But that's exactly like something Dan Smith would say. This is crazy! I wonder if Dan and Ally are still connected."

"I heard her on the phone this afternoon telling someone that I wasn't dead," Lana added.

"What? That does it! We're leaving here tonight. We'll drive into Nassau and spend the night. I don't feel it's safe for you to be here any longer."

"Are you going to question her?"

"Not yet. I'll get Tom to do a background check on her. But I don't want to alert her that anything's changed."

"How will you explain walking out on her dinner?"

"I guess we'll have to eat first. Then I'll come up with an excuse to leave." His ringing cell phone interrupted him. "Hi, Tom. What's up?" Tony spoke into the phone.

After listening and commenting a few times, he said to Tom, "Look, call me around eight o'clock so I can pretend there's an emergency that I need to get back to the states for. And as soon as you get a chance, do a background check on Ally Lawson.

**Tom had called as planned** with the trumped up emergency, and now Lana was in her room packing to leave. Too bad they had to cut their trip short. Lana loved this house.

Ally had prepared a wonderful meal for them, and was warm and accommodating the entire time. Lana didn't doubt for a minute that her change of attitude was because Tony was on the scene. She'd watched Ally and was convinced the woman was head over heels in love with Tony. No wonder she resented Lana.

Tony had said he'd knock on her door when he was ready to go, so with her bags packed and time to kill, Lana decided to strip the sheets off her bed. That would give her something to do while she waited.

She carefully folded the comforter and laid it in a chair. Then she pulled the top sheet off and tossed it to the floor. She was about to start taking the fitted sheet off the bed when she saw a black spot in the center of the bed. Leaning closer to see what it was, she jumped back in horror when she realized she was gazing at a black widow spider.

Her first impulse was to scream. She didn't consider herself arachnophobic, but she had a healthy hatred for the creatures. Especially if they were poisonous. But something stopped the scream before she let it out.

How did a black widow spider get into her bed? And had it been there while she'd slept? She knew it hadn't bitten her, because she would have been feeling the effects by now if it had.

Had someone put the spider in her bed? No! Surely not! The thought was not acceptable to Lana. And yet, someone had tried to kill her the night before. So maybe—would Ally go that far?

Lana rolled up a magazine, killed the offensive creature, and carefully placed it on the newspaper on the nightstand. If Ally had put the spider in her bed, she needed to know that it hadn't done its job.

**Tony had managed to book a flight** back to Mobile that night. On the plane, Lana told Tony everything that had happened the night before, including everything Tom had told her regarding Mary's death.

"I'd rather Tom hadn't told you as much as he did, but I guess if Dan made an attempt on your life, you need to know everything.

"Dan was brought in for questioning for Mary's death, but the authorities couldn't find any concrete evidence to charge him with, so they had to let him go. I've kept Tom on his trail ever since. Up until now he's led a very boring, non-eventful life. He does spend a lot of time following me, according to Tom. I couldn't figure that out, but now I'm wondering if he's just been waiting to see when I'd start seeing another woman. But that makes no sense at all."

"Unless he's determined that you don't have a successful love life," Lana said.

"He's one sick, vindictive son of a bitch if that's the case," Tony said. "But I know this—we have to watch you constantly so he doesn't get that close to you again."

"There was a black widow spider in my bed tonight," Lana said quietly.

"WHAT?" Tony bellowed, before lowering his voice again to the hushed tones they'd been using.

"I decided to take the sheets off my bed while I waited for you, and there was a black widow spider almost in the center of the bed, under the top sheet."

"That was put there by someone," Tony declared.

"I thought about that, but it could have crawled into the bed."

"No, Lana. I have that house sprayed for bugs, with emphasis on spiders and scorpions, once a month. Those are about the only poisonous bugs we have there, so I make sure I spray regularly for them.

"This has to mean that Ally is in with Dan Smith. Damn! I thought she was someone I could trust. I should have had a background check done on her before I hired her, but she had a good resume. But I can't fire her. That will alert them that we're on to her. I just can't take you back to the house until we get to the bottom of this.

"I knew she didn't like Mary, but Mary could be very demanding, so I thought there was just a personality conflict."

The plane was landing, so there wasn't time for further talk until they were in Tony's black Mercedes.

"You must prefer black vehicles," Lana said.

"They get less attention," was the simple answer, before his cell phone started ringing. "Tony," he answered the phone. After listening for a few minutes, he said, "Thanks, Tom. You did a fantastic job, as usual. We're back in Mobile, and I'm trying to decide what to do with Lana. But I'll keep you informed. Thanks again."

"You're trying to decide what to do with Lana?" she asked, trying to keep the indignation from her voice.

"Ally is Dan Smith's cousin. Their moms were sisters. Ally's parents raised Dan. So I'm sure they're in this together. Whatever 'this' is," Tony said, and turned the car in the opposite direction of Lana's house.

# Chapter 7

**"Where are you going?"** Lana asked. "This isn't the way to my house."

"I think it's best if you stay with me for a while until we figure out what Dan is up to."

"And when were you going to ask me if that's what I want to do?" Lana liked Tony a lot, but she wasn't ready to let him start making decisions for her. Were Italian males really as domineering as the movies depicted them? She'd never gotten that impression from Tony, but she'd soon find out.

"Take me home. I'm not going to hide out from some kook."

"You don't understand, Lana. I believe Dan killed Mary. And it's obvious he tried to kill you. This isn't something we can play around with. He's more than just a kook, as you call him."

"I know he meant to kill me. I saw the actual pleasure in his eyes when he thought I would die. And I saw the malice on his face when he shot Tom. In fact, I wonder if he knew who Tom was and tried to kill him on purpose."

"Hmmm. I never thought of that," Tony said. "You may be right. That's very perceptive of you." He reached for his cell phone. "Tom? Lana just came up with a thought that I haven't considered. She thinks Dan may have known who you were and tried to kill you on purpose. Did you get any vibes like that?" Tony listened for several minutes before disconnecting the phone.

"Tom said he'd wondered about it, since Dan was so quick to shoot him. But now he thinks Dan was just trying to eliminate any witnesses. He probably meant to kill whoever drove the boat to meet him. But why is Dan doing this?"

"Hate can make some people crazy," Lana said. "Maybe he hates you enough that he's determined you'll never be happy. If he's miserable, he wants to make sure you stay miserable."

They'd stopped at a traffic light at a major intersection. Lana knew the loop would take them back toward her house, so she said, "Tony, I'm serious. I want to go home. I have to get back to work, and I don't plan to commute from your house. I live much closer to See the World."

"Lana—"

"Take a left, Tony, and take me home. I'm kind of put-out with you right now, because you didn't ask my opinion on this. You just took it upon yourself to take control of my life. I don't like that, and you should know it up front."

She expected anything but the loud laugh that exploded from him, and the fact that he actually turned the car left when the light changed.

"Now that's what Italian men like!" he said. "Strong women who stand up to them! Damn, you're sexy! I'm tempted to pull over and make love to you in the middle of all this traffic. You think we could get away with it?" His teasing eyes lingered on her face before going back to his driving.

"We'd probably get thrown in jail. That's all I need, to get arrested as a hooker!"

"Well, at least you'd be safe in jail," Tony said, becoming serious again. "Promise me you'll be aware of everything around you when I'm not with you. Don't take any chances, and don't go *anywhere* at night alone, okay?"

"Okay, Tony. I've got Mace in my purse. I'll keep it close and spray it on anyone who dares get close to me!" Lana replied.

Tony pulled the car into Lana's driveway and turned to her. "I don't get the feeling you're taking this as seriously as you should, Lana. It really isn't a joking matter."

"I know it's serious, Tony. Remember, I'm the one who almost died out in that boat and storm. But I refuse to let someone terrorize me into changing my lifestyle! By not running and hiding, I'm telling anyone who might be watching that they aren't in control of my life."

Tony laced his fingers through the hair at the nape of her neck and drew her close. "You're not only good to look at, you're the most stubborn, brave woman I've ever known," he said before capturing her lips in his.

"And you taste good, too," he said with his lips still against hers. "You've invaded my blood. My senses. You're in my every waking moment. I don't want to let you go. I resent the fact that our time in the Bahamas was cut short. Why don't you come on home with me and we won't let anyone know we're back. We'll just finish out our two weeks' vacation at my house."

Lana gazed into Tony's eyes and was tempted by his suggestion. It made sense. And after all, she was in his house in the Bahamas. What was the difference?

Her mom was the difference. Her mom hadn't known she was going to be staying in Tony's house in the Bahamas. She had probably assumed they'd be in a hotel with separate bedrooms. And while she did have her own bedroom at his house in the Bahamas, there was a difference in being here in Mobile and staying in his house. Sure, it was an old-fashioned viewpoint, but her mom was old-fashioned in many ways.

"I think my mom would frown upon that idea, Tony," she said.

"Lana, you're a grown woman. You can't spend your life trying to please your mom," he reasoned.

"I know, but tonight I'm too tired to make a life-changing decision," she said, and reached for the door handle.

She unlocked the front door of her house, and Tony followed her inside, closing it behind them. "So if you won't come to my house, I'll just stay with you," he announced, making himself at home on her couch.

"You know, you're becoming pushy all of a sudden. We need to

talk abut this," she said. "But first I have to go to the bathroom."
She left him with a lopsided grin on his face.

"TONY!"

Lana's frightened voice sent Tony in a run to her.

She stood immobile, staring at the mirror that ran the entire length of her bathroom sink and vanity. Bright red lipstick
had been used to write "IF YOU WANT TO LIVE STAY AWAY
FROM HIM" in huge letters. The discarded tube of lipstick lay on
the countertop.

"Did you touch anything?" Tony asked, leading her back to the
living room.

"No," she said. "I just walked in and there it was."

Tony was in the process of dialing 911 even as she answered
him. He gave the address to her house, then sat beside her on the
couch.

"Now are you convinced that you're in danger?" he asked, taking her trembling hands in his and holding them tightly.

"I'm convinced that there's one sick person on the loose," she
answered, and rested her head on the wide shoulder he offered.
"But when did this happen? If it was Dan, did he somehow know
that we'd come back here? Did he rush back and do this, or did he
do it before he followed us to the Bahamas?"

"Assuming that it was Dan who did this, I don't know the answers to your questions. Maybe Tom can shed some light on Dan's
activities." He reached for his cell phone. It only took a few minutes for Tom to assure Tony that Dan was still in the Bahamas.
Tony explained to Tom what they had just found.

"So who was it? Does this mean he has an accomplice?" Lana
asked.

But the arriving police cars interrupted any answer Tony may
have offered.

**After an hour of inspecting the house** and asking Lana and Tony
many questions, the police found nothing that could give them
any clues of who had been in her house. Since the lipstick wasn't
Lana's, they took the empty tube with them. It was their only evi-

dence, even though it had no fingerprints on it.

But the most puzzling part was that there was no sign of forced entry. The police insisted that whoever was in the house had come in through a door, so they must have a key.

As Tony said final goodbyes to the police, Lana puzzled over who had been able to just walk into her house. Her mom and Jenny were the only two people who had keys to her house. Ron didn't even have a key, but he knew where the one was hidden on the patio—

She'd forgotten about the key on the patio!

"There's a key on the patio I forgot about," Lana said as Tony came back inside. He followed her through the sliding glass doors that led to the patio from her dining area.

She went to the rock wall that outlined the patio and counted five stones from the inside corner. With both hands, she carefully pulled a rock from its resting place. If one didn't know the rock was loose, it would never be detected.

"It's gone," Lana said. "The key is gone. So whoever took it still has it."

"Which means they can come and go into your house anytime they want to," Tony said. "Who knew about this key?"

"Ron."

"Anyone else? Have you ever casually mentioned to anyone that you keep a key hidden out here?"

"No. I've made sure that I don't mention it. And I made Ron promise not to tell anyone. But maybe he just let it slip to someone. Should we call the police and let them know?"

"Yes. I'll do that tomorrow. Also, we need to change the locks on all the doors in the morning."

"I'm staying here tonight, in case they come back," Lana said. Her lifted chin and the stubborn look challenged Tony to argue with her.

But he didn't argue. Instead he wrapped his arms around her and drew her close. "You're something else," he whispered, pressing his cheek against her hair. "Your bravery just makes me want to take care of you all the more. Okay, we'll stay here tonight."

"You don't have to stay, Tony. My guest bed isn't all that comfortable," she said, relishing the reassurance of being held close to him.

"I'll make do with it. Surely you know I wouldn't leave you alone now. Do you want to call your mom tonight or wait until in the morning?"

"I'll wait. No need to worry her over something she can't fix. She has your cell phone number, if she needs us."

"Do you want to go out and get a bite to eat? Or we can have pizza delivered, if you'd prefer." Tony's arms still held her close. Lana didn't want to break the moment, but reluctantly, she did.

"You know what? Right now the thing I want the most is to get a shower and get into something more comfortable. Can we wait that long to make a decision on the food?"

A wicked grin curved Tony's lips. "Well, depending on what you decide is comfortable clothing, we might just prolong the food decision for a while!"

"I didn't mean *that* comfortable," Lana chided. "I just want to get out of these clothes I've traveled in all day."

The disappointed look on Tony's face brought a gurgle of laughter from her. "You have a one-track mind, don't you?" she said.

"I told you. When it comes to you, I do. I can't think of anything else when you're around."

"In that case, I'd better get out of your sight. I'll be in the shower," she said, heading down the hallway that led to her room.

"And who says you'll be safe in the shower?"

Tony's words brought the happenings of the night back to her, and she turned to face him with apprehension on her face.

"I meant from me, sweetheart! You're safe from everybody but me, tonight," he said, coming to her and pulling her close again.

They stood at the doorway of the main bathroom, where the warning had been written. The police had made an attempt at cleaning the lipstick off the mirror, but as Lana glanced in the door she could still see red traces on the glass.

Tony felt the shudder that went through her and glanced up to notice what she'd seen. He quickly led her down the hallway to her bedroom door. "Get your shower. I'll go make some coffee while I wait for you."

Lana sat on the side of her bed and glanced around the familiar room, which now felt strange. Just knowing someone had been in her home destroyed the calm she'd always felt when she was here. Would she ever feel safe again? Lana wasn't easily frightened, but the last couple of days had made her feel very vulnerable.

But she would not give in to it! Renewed determination set in and she went to her chest of drawers to get clean underwear. She stared at an empty drawer.

Quickly pulling open the other drawers, she found that they were all empty. All her panties, bras, and sleepwear were gone!

The police had checked her room for any foul play, just like they'd checked the rest of the house. But she didn't know if they'd opened any of the drawers. And how about the closet?

She went to the closet and checked her clothes. Everything seemed to be just as she'd left it. Chills ran up and down her spine as she left her room and hurried back to Tony.

"Tony, I think we'd better call Mom. I don't think I want to spend the night here," she said, collapsing into a dining room chair and cupping her face in her hands.

Tony abandoned his coffeemaking and rushed to her. "Lana! What's wrong? What happened?"

Her entire body was visibly shaking. "Someone has stolen all my underwear and sleepwear."

# Chapter 8

**Alma set coffee down** in front of Tony and Lana, then brought a cup for herself. It had the makings of a long night. They sat around her dining room table after Lana and Tony had arrived at her home.

"Okay, tell me everything that's happened," she said.

Lana told her mom about her ordeal on the boat, the spider in her bed, and the latest, coming home to find someone had been in her house. Tony filled in the gaps that Lana left out.

Finally Alma turned to Tony and said, "I know it's still hard for you to talk about this, but Tony, it's obvious you're getting involved with my daughter, so don't you think it's time you told us about your wife? Don't you think Lana has the right to know a little about your situation, if she's falling in love with you?"

"Mom!" Lana protested.

"Shush, child. I see the way you look at him. Anyone can tell you're head over heels for him. Now you two have brought this home to me, so that opens the door for me to get involved as a mother. And Lana, you know I'm not going to stand by and watch you get hurt emotionally without saying something. And I'm sure not going to stand by and watch you get murdered!"

"You're right, Alma, you're right," Tony said. "It's time you two know the entire story."

So for a while he repeated the part of his life that Lana had heard from Tom and Ally. "But what Tom doesn't even know," he said, turning to Lana, "is that Mary and I were having a lot of trouble before she died. She turned out to be a very clinging wife. And she got worse after Gino was born." His voice quavered when he spoke his son's name.

"She didn't want me going on any business trips. She wanted me home to help take care of 'the little brat,' as she called him." There was a bitterness in his voice that Lana had never heard before.

Tony paused for several seconds, lost in unpleasant memories. Finally he continued. "She'd started threatening to leave me. And in one of her fits of anger, she mentioned taking her own life. But after I questioned her about it, she promised she'd never go that far."

"Do you think she was having an affair?" Lana asked.

"I don't know. I really don't think so, but I have no way of knowing for sure. I don't believe she was seeing Dan. She genuinely hated the man."

"Tom mentioned that the fire was caused from cigarettes. Do you think she'd started smoking?" Lana asked.

"If Mary had started smoking, then she was the biggest hypocrite on the face of the earth. She really got volatile when someone lit a cigarette around her. She gave every indication of hating them. That's why I was so surprised when the cause of fire was determined to be from her smoking in bed. There's just no way."

"Do you think she set the house on fire on purpose with the cigarettes, and followed through with her threat to kill herself?" Alma asked.

This was obviously a question Tony hadn't considered, from the look on his face. "Surely she wouldn't choose so painful a death as burning!" he said. "No. Mary didn't like pain. She wouldn't have done that to herself, and hopefully, she wouldn't have done it to Gino."

"Did they find their remains?" Alma asked.

"They never found any of Mary's body. But Gino—they suspect he died of smoke inhalation, but his little body was badly burned." Tony stopped and cupped his face in his hands. His shoulders shook with emotion.

Lana went to him and wrapped her arms around him. "Tony, don't. Please don't cry. We don't have to talk about this anymore tonight."

"Let's just try to get some sleep, and we can start over in the morning," Alma said. "Tony, you take the guest room. It's at the end of the hallway. There's a full bath joining the guestroom, so you'll have a lot of privacy."

"I hate to mess up your room for just one night. I should just go on home," he said, standing as if to leave.

"I think you both should stay here for a few days," Alma suggested. "That way, nobody will know where you are. It will throw anyone off who might be following you."

"Alma, you're a saint of a woman, but I can't put you in that kind of danger," Tony said.

"You already have. By getting involved with my daughter, you've put her in danger. And by putting her in danger, you've automatically put me in danger." There were no accusations in Alma's voice. Just facts.

"You're right," Tony said, slumping back into his chair. "But you have to believe I never dreamed anything like this would happen! I never imagined Dan Smith would try to harm another woman I became involved with."

"So you haven't dated anyone since Mary died?" Alma asked.

"No. Lana's the first woman who has attracted my attention in years. And that includes Mary. I thought I was in love with Mary when we were in college, but it didn't take long for that to wear off. But I wanted to stay married for Gino's sake.

"Since Mary died, I've barely looked at another woman. Then I walked in here a few weeks ago and saw Lana and she knocked me off my feet." He was talking to Alma, but was staring deeply into Lana's eyes.

"Well," Alma said, interrupting the long look between the two who had forgotten she was in the room, "I do wish you'd stay here until this is solved. I'd feel a lot better about both of you if I knew where you were."

"Let me sleep on it. I'll give you my decision in the morning," he said.

"Mom, I really don't see the reason for us to bring this to your house." Lana finally put her thoughts into the conversation. "You know I hate running from a situation."

"This isn't running, Lana. It's outsmarting the enemy for a little while. Maybe long enough for the police to get to the bottom of what's going on," Alma argued.

"Whether I stay or not, I want you to stay with your mom," Tony said.

"Look, you two. I'm a big girl! I can take care of myself! I don't need to be smothered."

"That's enough, Lana!" Alma finally gave way to the emotions she'd tried to hide since she'd heard about her daughter almost losing her life. "If it hadn't been for this Tom fellow, you'd be at the bottom of the ocean in the Bahamas right now! So don't try to be such an island!" Tears streamed down her face as she came and wrapped her arms around Lana.

"Oh, Mom! I'm sorry. I know this is hard on you. Okay, if it'll make you feel better, I'll stay here until we find out what's going on."

"Thank you, baby. At least I can sleep at night if I know you're here with me."

**Later, snuggling into her old bed,** Lana looked around the room where she'd spent so many happy years. Her parents had bought this house when she and Jenny were small. This had been her safe haven for almost as long as she could remember. The same feeling of security tried to settle around her, but kept getting interrupted by flashes of Dan Smith's maniacal face as he abandoned her in the ocean.

Finally she dozed off, only to come awake with the red lipstick message screaming across her mind. She went to her bathroom and took a couple of over-the-counter pain pills, hoping they would relax her enough so she could get some sleep.

After turning and tossing a little while longer, she finally drifted into a troubled sleep, only to dream about running from dark shadows and unknown dangers.

**The heavenly aroma of coffee** brought her slowly awake. Glancing at the clock on the bedside table, she saw that it was seven o'clock. Her mom would have been up for at least an hour. Even though it was Saturday, Alma got up at the same time every day.

Donning a robe, Lana headed toward the kitchen. She was eager to get her day started. Eager to find out who was going and coming in her home when they pleased. Eager to be out of the bed that turned out to be her enemy for the night instead of the friend she was used to.

She found Alma and Tony in the sunroom, both holding a steaming cup of coffee.

"Did you sleep well?" Alma asked, pouring Lana some coffee from the carafe that sat on the table between her and Tony.

"Like a baby," Lana lied. "How about you two?"

"So-so," Alma answered. "I kept having bad dreams."

"I'm sorry, Mom. I wish you'd never had to be involved in this."

"Don't be silly. I have to be involved in this."

"How did you sleep on the guest bed, Tony? It's not the best bed in the world," Lana sympathized.

"The bed is fine, but like Alma, I had troubling dreams," Tony answered. "But there was one time during the early morning hours that car lights were shining in my window. Do you have a neighbor who comes home late and lets their lights shine over here?"

"The house that would face that bedroom window is empty," Alma said. "There's no reason a car should even be over there."

"The car sat there for about thirty minutes. I kept looking at the clock wondering if the lights were ever going to go off. I thought it might be a car that the lights go off automatically. Then I wondered if someone had forgotten to turn them off. By the time I got frustrated enough to get up and try to see what was going on, the car left. We'll see if it happens again tonight."

"That's strange," Alma said. "Like I said, the house has been empty for a while."

"So you're going to stay here?" Lana asked.

"Yes. I think so, for the safety of you and your mom, and as she suggested, it might help confuse whoever was in your house, or whoever might be following us. I think we need to stash my car somewhere, though. It won't serve any purpose if one of them discovers all our cars here."

"Where would you leave your car?" Alma asked.

"Lana and I could drop it off at the airport long-term parking and leave it there for a few days. I'll rent a car to drive. Maybe we could do that after we talk with the police this morning," he said, turning to Lana.

"Sure. In the meantime, I need to get back in the attic and get more clothes. I think I've outgrown what I took with me on the trip."

"Your body is hurrying to get back to its natural weight, isn't it, darling?" Alma said, placing her hand over Lana's. "You were starving yourself. I'm so happy you decided to stop that. I was really worried about you. I've been afraid you'd become anorexic or bulimic."

"Well, Mom, you never had to worry about me being bulimic. I don't like throwing up or the effects of laxatives. I prefer to just go hungry. But not anymore. I've given you my word on that."

"Lana, why don't you let me take you shopping at Angelino's today? Just give your old clothes to your favorite charity and get some new ones."

"Tony! I can't afford the clothes at Angelino's. And besides, there's no reason to buy new clothes until I settle at the weight I'm going to be. That would just be throwing money to the wind."

"But we have some wonderful sales going on. And the clothes wouldn't cost you a penny.  I want to do this for you."

"You're too kind, Tony. But there's no need to give away what I have until I get a little more use out of them." Lana had never been a spendthrift.

"Lana, why don't you take him up on his offer?" Alma said.

"About all that's left in the attic are older things. You need some new, modern outfits to celebrate your 'coming out.'"

"See, you're outvoted," Tony teased.

Reluctantly Lana gave in. She helped her mom prepare breakfast, then she and Tony headed for her house to meet with the police.

When they left her mom's, neither of them noticed the leering face in the window of the empty house next door.

# Chapter 9

"The detective said your fingerprints were the only ones on the door jambs," Tony said. "So whoever went inside your house wore gloves. Which means they were up to no good."

Reality finally, completely settled in for Lana. Someone was threatening her. Leaving the Bahamas had given her a false sense that she'd left the danger there. But the threat was following her. Someone was deliberately stalking her. Someone had been in her house. Her *home*.

And somehow, that person had to be connected to Ron. He was the only one, other than her mom, who knew about the key.

Fear engulfed Lana. Anger promptly replaced the fear.

Lana had gotten into several sticky situations because her "flight" response immediately gave place to her "fight" instincts. Lana never ran. And she wasn't running from this. But she *would* get to the bottom of it.

Taking her cell phone from her purse, she dialed Ron's number. "When can I see you?" she asked. She waited for his answer, then said, "Okay, how about three o'clock at my house?"

"Lana! I don't think that's a very good idea," Tony said. "Why would you meet him at your house, if he knows what happened?"

"I can't believe that Ron is in on this. But I want to find out if he's told anyone about the key."

"Then I'll be with you when you see him."

"No. There are some other things that Ron and I need to get out in the open, and I know he won't talk if you're there."

"Lana—"

"Tony, I'll be fine. Ron won't hurt me."

"You are one stubborn woman, Lana Clarke," Tony said.

"I know. That's why you love me," Lana said. *Where did that come from?* she thought, mortified that she'd said it. But maybe Tony hadn't heard, because he didn't comment. Or maybe he just didn't want to comment.

He pulled the car into a reserved spot in front of Angelino's and killed the engine, then turned to Lana. "Your stubbornness is only one of the things that I love about you. I love the way your eyes flash when you're angry. I love the way they turn to liquid pools of blue softness when you're feeling amorous. I love your soft lips and the way they feel under mine. I love your hair blowing in the wind. And that body! Your body makes my blood run hot! And I want nothing more than to make love to you right now, but since the surveillance cameras are on us, we'd better just go inside and shop for your clothes."

Melting from the inside out, Lana followed Tony into the swanky department store. His words filled her mind with longing, but one fact remained uppermost. In all his sweet words, he didn't say he loved *her*. Just things *about* her. And that could just be attributed to attraction, not love.

*Well, it's a little early in the relationship to be declaring love, don't you think?* a reasoning voice inside her head reminded her. *Do you love him?*

"Lana?"

Startled out of her reverie, Lana realized that a saleslady had walked up, and one of them must have asked her a question. "I'm sorry. I was so lost in admiring the store I wasn't paying attention."

"Maggie was saying that these are the clothes she put on the racks for you to pick from. She's placed them close to the fitting rooms so you don't have to walk back and forth." Tony indicated three large racks filled with every style for any occasion that anyone could possibly need. "Pick out any and every thing you want, Lana. Don't just get what you think you need. Get things you *want*."

"Tony. I've told you this is a waste of money. I'll just pick out a few things for now, because I know I'll need more later."

Tony placed his hands on each side of her face and gazed into her eyes. "I knew you were going to be difficult about this. As I said, you're a stubborn woman. But you need to learn a lesson today. I'm more stubborn than you could ever dream to be. You'll only win an argument that I allow you to win." And right in the middle of his declaration, right in front of Maggie, one of his top supervisors, he captured Lana's lips in a long, tender kiss.

When he ended the kiss, he turned to Maggie. "Since she's not going to cooperate, just have everything on these racks packed up and sent to the address I gave you earlier. We'll bring back the things she doesn't like."

"Tony!" Lana started to protest, but he took her arm and said, "Come on. I want you to meet someone."

They were passing through the men's department when Lana suddenly stopped and ducked behind a tall rack of overcoats, pulling Tony with her. "Look at that woman talking with the salesman," she said.

"That's Julian. He's one of my managers," Tony said. "She looks familiar. Do we know her?"

"Isn't that Maxie? She's the woman who was having lunch at Alfonzo's with Ron."

"Hmm. It does look like her. But so what? She's just shopping. I hope she's not talking with Julian because she has a problem with something. He's my head manager."

"Look at the expression on their faces. They don't look like a manager and customer discussing a clothing problem."

"You're right. Something does seem amiss. You stay here and I'll try to get close enough to hear the conversation. Not that I'd spy on my employees under normal circumstances. But this doesn't seem normal."

Lana watched from her vantage point as Tony made his way within a few feet of his manager and Maxie. They were so intent on their conversation that they didn't notice him. Finally Maxie slipped the manager a white envelope and quickly left the store. Julian turned and hurried away.

"Very interesting," Tony said as he and Lana met in the aisle. "It was apparently some kind of payoff. I could only hear bits and pieces of the conversation, but I heard Maxie saying things like 'good job,' and 'earned this,' and once she said something that sounded like my name, but I wasn't sure. Then she handed him an envelope that was thick with papers or money."

"Is Julian married? Maybe they're married and getting a divorce. That could be what the papers are," Lana offered.

"Julian doesn't care for women. He prefers men," Tony said.

"Oh. Then I guess that blows that theory out the window."

Lana couldn't shake the gnawing feeling she'd had while watching Maxie. Like something she was trying to remember, but wouldn't quite come to the forefront of her mind.

**After leaving Tony at a rental car office,** Lana headed to her house to meet with Ron.

She wandered around her house while she waited for him. Everything that should feel normal seemed odd to her. She felt like a stranger in her own home. As if she didn't belong. She felt invaded. Her place of comfort had been tainted.

The loud knocking on the front door startled her. "Lana?" Ron called.

"Hi, Ron," she said, opening the door for him.

"Hi, baby," Ron said, trying to take her in his arms.

But Lana evaded his embrace and walked across the room in pretense of straightening a picture on the wall.

"Lana? What's wrong?"

"When I got back from a trip last night, someone had been in my house. Someone had written a warning to me on my bathroom mirror. They also took all my underwear, which is very strange. That someone had used the key I keep hidden in the patio wall. And they didn't return the key. You're the only one who knows about the key. Did you tell anyone about the key, Ron?"

"I'm sorry. I have the key in my pocket. I meant to bring it back the next day, but just forgot about it. Here it is," he said, handing the key to her.

"So what were you doing in my house while I was away?"

"I wanted to borrow a couple of your CDs. I was entertaining at my place and wanted some soft mood music, and I knew you had several easy listening artists that I like. I didn't think you'd mind."

"Let me get this straight. After we've dated for a year, you decide to borrow some of my CDs to play for one of your dates and you didn't think I'd mind?"

"Well, after all, you were traipsing around the world with a man who isn't exactly a father figure to you. Am I supposed to mind that?"

"Touché, Ron. But did you tell your friend about the key, or did she see you take it?"

"It was Maxie. You've met her. She was supposed to stay in the car, but after I got in the house, she came in and said she needed to use the bathroom. Was I supposed to tell her to hold it?"

"Did you go in the bathroom after she'd been?"

"No. As soon as she finished, we left."

"So she didn't see you take the key from the hiding place? And you didn't tell her about it?"

"No, Lana. I'd never betray your trust like that."

Suddenly the nagging feeling Lana had felt when she was watching Maxie and Julian in the store came to the forefront. Her bright red lipstick! That had been the same color lipstick on her bathroom mirror.

"Ron, I think Maxie may be mixed up with some really bad people. You might not want to get too involved with her."

"Now this is a good sign! You're jealous. That makes me happy, Lana," he said, moving to her again.

But Lana stopped him at arm's length. "Ron, I think it was Maxie who wrote a threatening note on my bathroom mirror. It was written with the same color lipstick she wears."

"No way! Maxie is too sweet to do something like that! I don't know who was in your house, but I'd bet my life it wasn't Maxie."

Ron's defense was strong, so Lana decided not to tell him anything about her close encounter with death in the Bahamas.
"Just be careful, okay? I would hate for you to get involved with the wrong crowd."

"You sound like my mom. I don't need another mom. I need my girl back."

"Let's save that discussion for a later time, okay? I've got some errands to run that can't wait."

"When, Lana? When can we have that discussion?"

"Have you decided you can live with a fat woman? Have you decided that you love me no matter what size I am? If so, why are you dating a tall, slim woman?"

"I didn't say I was dating Maxie. I said I was entertaining her."

"Oh. My mistake. Of course, there's a difference?"

"All I did was have her over to my apartment and cook a nice meal for her. That's entertaining. We didn't jump in bed when it was over."

"Too bad. You might have enjoyed it." Lana said, sitting down in her car.

"Lana—"

"Later, Ron. I have to go now."

"Are you staying here alone? I don't like that idea, if someone's threatening you. Do you want me to stay with you?"

"No, I'll be fine," she answered. She didn't feel free to tell him she was staying at her mom's.

As she watched him get into his car and drive away, she wondered if he knew more than he was telling. Because even if Maxie had sneaked into her bathroom and written on her mirror, how would she have managed to empty two chests of drawers and take the contents from the house without Ron knowing it?

And if Maxie didn't do it, then who did?

**As she pulled up in front of her mom's house,** she saw a strange car parked in the driveway and assumed it was Tony's rental. There were no rental signs on it. Smart man. Cover his tracks.

But as she entered the house, she recognized Jenny's and Hank's voices coming from the kitchen. *Great*, she thought. Now she'd have to hear Jenny's take on her new weight gain. She wished she could be excited to see her sister, but Jenny made it hard to be excited to see her. Hank must be a saint to love Jenny like he did.

"Is that you, Lana?" Alma called from the kitchen. "We're in here having some iced tea."

"Okay, Mom," Lana called back, and headed for the kitchen. The dining room and kitchen were together, but for some reason, they always just referred to it as the kitchen.

"Hi, Jenny. Hi, Hank." Lana said, entering the room. "Who got a new car?"

"Hi, Lana," Hank said, smiling and standing to give her a hug. "That would be me with the new ride. You look beautiful, as ever."

"Oh my! It's sure not taking you long to put that weight back on, is it?" Jenny said, not making a move to hug Lana.

"Jenny! Is it impossible for you to be polite to your sister?" Alma scolded.

"It's okay, Mom. I was expecting it. It really doesn't matter," Lana said, just wanting to move on past this part of the meeting.

"That's the problem, I think," Jenny pushed on. "The fact that it doesn't matter is why it's so easy for you to let yourself go. If it mattered to you—if *we*, your loved ones, mattered to you, you'd want to take better care of yourself."

"Jenny, drop this right now," Alma said. "I mean it. Drop it!"

Before Jenny could respond they heard the front door opening. "Hello?" Tony called.

Alma had insisted that Tony have his own key and was to come and go as he pleased, for as long as he stayed there.

"In here!" Lana and Alma chorused.

Tony appeared at the doorway, loaded down with packages. "Your new wardrobe, madam," Tony said to Lana. "Where would you like them?"

"In my bedroom, please," she answered.

"Oh my! You must have bought out the store!" Jenny said.

"Actually, this is only part of what she has," Tony said. "There's much more in the car outside." And he headed to Lana's room to deposit his bundles.

"Did you strike a goldmine?" Jenny asked.

"No. Not exactly," Lana hedged, not wanting to get into the whole free-clothes-from-Tony thing.

"Well, what? And why are you buying so many clothes now? You know you're just going to get fatter and outgrow them."

"These clothes are from Tony's store. They're seasonal and on sale, so Tony just gave them to Lana," Alma explained.

"Oh. He really is enabling her to get fat, isn't he? I just didn't figure Tony to be one of those weird guys who likes fat women."

"Jenny, honey, why don't you just let up some?" Hank finally stepped in. "A guy doesn't have to be weird to like a voluptuous woman."

"Oh, great! Don't tell me you like fat women, too!" Jenny turned on Hank with disdain in her eyes.

"It's not a size that I like in a woman. It's her personality. Who she is. I don't care what size she is. For instance, you may gain weight after we're married, and that won't bother me a bit," he said.

"Oh, you can bet your life I'll never be fat!" Jenny all but screamed. "I would rather be dead!"

"Jenny?" Tony's quiet voice came from the doorway where he'd been leaning, unnoticed, against the door jamb, listening to the conversation. "First, as Hank said, a man isn't weird just because he's attracted to a certain body type. If I liked extremely thin women, you wouldn't think I was weird. If I liked older women, you wouldn't think I was weird. I just don't understand the reasoning that when a man is attracted to a larger woman, he automatically becomes weird, or has some kind of fetish. Frankly, I think that's narrow-mindedness at its worst.

"And you know what else I think? I think you have a fear of fat. I think that's why you're so hard on Lana. You're afraid if she doesn't control her weight, somehow that will translate to you and you'll become fat. Is that true, Jenny?"

"Well, we all know what happened to poor Tommy Henning," Jenny said, barely controlling the emotion in her voice.

Suddenly understanding dawned for Lana and Alma as they exchanged glances.

Tommy Henning had been in Jenny's class in high school. He'd been a very heavy child and had gotten continually larger in his teen years. After taking all the harsh ribbing he could stand, he'd committed suicide when he was in the tenth grade.

Jenny had been the only person who'd befriended Tommy during those years. She'd seen and heard all the mean things that were done and said to him. And his death had been extremely hard on her.

"Oh, honey. I'm sorry. I should have remembered Tommy. I should have known how his life and death had affected you," Alma said, putting her arms around Jenny's shoulders.

"But what I don't understand is why you say the same things to me that you hated for people to say to Tommy. That doesn't make any sense," Lana said.

"I thought if I said them to you it would make you stay on your diet and you wouldn't have to hear those mean words from strangers," Jenny said, reaching for Lana's hand.

"So you were trying to protect me?"

"Yes."

"Who was Tommy Henning?" Tony asked.

"He was my childhood sweetheart," Jenny said, weeping into her hands. "He was the man I planned to marry."

# Chapter 10

**Lana and Alma stared at Jenny** in disbelief. They knew she'd spent a lot of time with Tommy, but neither had a clue that she'd imagined herself in love with him.

"Jenny, I didn't know," Alma said.

Hank pulled Jenny to him and held her as she spilled her pent-up emotions.

"I know, Mom. I didn't tell a soul. But Tommy was the most caring, thoughtful, forgiving person I've ever known." She used a cloth napkin to try to contain the flow of tears that kept coming. Once the dam had broken it didn't want to stop. "Even when those horrible kids made fun of him, he'd tell me that they didn't understand and they were just repeating what they'd been taught. Then he'd smile at me and tell me that I was his only friend and how he appreciated and loved me.

"Then when his doctor and his mom put him on those diet pills, he began to change. He started withdrawing from life. From me. He became more and more depressed. He started saying things like 'someone like me doesn't deserve to be on this earth,' and that he'd 'be better off dead. That everyone would be better off' if he were dead. When I kept on trying to encourage him, he told me that I didn't understand how it felt to be fat. That I'd always been slim and didn't have a clue how he felt.

"I tried to tell his mom that I thought the diet pills were making him depressed, but she told me to mind my own business and stop meddling. She asked me if I thought I knew more than Tommy's doctor.

"Then they found him—they found him dead because he'd taken an overdose of the diet pills." Overcome again, Jenny cried into the tear-soaked napkin.

"Here, use this," Alma said, handing her a wet bath cloth. "Wipe your face, honey."

Jenny took the cloth and wiped her face and slowly contained her tears. "I should have done more to help him, Mom. I could have done *something*."

"You were his friend. You tried to help him. You *did* help him by standing beside him. But we can't make our friends and loved ones do things they don't want to do. He had the influence of his mom and doctor working against you. Plus he wanted to believe that the pills would help. He wanted to believe he could be different than he was. You must never feel guilty for his death, Jenny. You did all you could do."

"Thanks, Mom. I'm sorry for falling apart." Turning to Lana, she said, "Please forgive me for being so mean to you. I love you so much, and I was afraid I'd lose you like I lost Tommy."

Lana went to Jenny and wrapped her arms around her. "Dear, dear Jenny. I'm not going anywhere. I'm your big sister. I plan to be here a long time and boss you around like any big sister is supposed to do!"

After hugging Lana and Alma, Jenny turned to Hank and said, "Will you take me home? I think I've destroyed the wedding planning mood for today. I guess we'll have to try again later."

After they'd left, Alma said, "Poor Jenny. I'm her mom. I should have been more in tune to her feelings for Tommy, and especially her grief after he died."

"Now, Alma, follow your own advice to Jenny," Tony said. "Don't blame yourself for something you couldn't help. Jenny only let you see what she wanted you to see. She seems like a very private person to me. She kept her emotions from you on purpose, so don't beat yourself up."

"How did you get so wise, Tony? You're right, of course," Alma agreed.

"I'm not wise, Alma. But I spent a lot of time in therapy after my wife and son were killed. I had to work through a lot of baggage."

Tony's cell phone rang, so he excused himself from the room to take the call.

"I've got some errands to run," Alma said to Lana. "Then I'll stop by the grocery store on my way home. So I may be gone for a few hours, in case you start to wonder about me."

"I have to go to the office, ladies. It seems I have an emergency that only I can handle. I don't know how long it will take," Tony said, coming to Lana and drawing her close.

"*Tony*," Lana whispered, indicating her mom with her eyes.

"What?" he asked, lowering his lips to hers in a light, affectionate kiss. "Stay in the house while I'm gone," he said with his lips still close to hers. "I don't want you taking any chances."

Lana pulled away from him, glancing guiltily at her mom, who had a wide grin on her face. "I'll be fine, Tony. You two go do what you have to do. I'm going to look at my new clothes."

"You mean you're leaving, too?" Tony asked Alma.

"Yes, I have some errands."

"Then you come with me, Lana. I don't want you to be alone for awhile."

"Tony! Lighten up! I'm not going to be a prisoner, and I don't need a bodyguard. We've been through this. We're only talking about a few hours, here. Now go do your job. Mom, do your errands. Goodbye!" She left them staring after her as she left the room.

**In her room,** Lana finally heard the front door close and assumed both of them had left. She looked at the boxes Tony had stacked around her bed. She barely had room to walk.

One thing was for sure. She didn't have room for all these clothes in her closet, even if it was a large walk-in. She'd just hang a few of the items in this closet, then take the rest of the clothes to her house.

She didn't plan on hiding out at her mom's much longer anyway. Especially after she went back to work in a few days. She just couldn't see the need for it. If someone wanted to find her, they'd find her no matter where she was.

**Across the street,** in the empty house, two sets of eyes met. "She didn't go with either of them, did she?"

"Nope. She's alone."

**Lana busily went through all the boxes** of clothes. She was amazed at the things Tony had picked out for her. All the colors were perfect. He had a good eye for color. And they all seemed to be a perfect fit, although she didn't try on everything. Just a few of the items that took her breath away.

She stood in front of her bathroom mirror looking at herself in a red pantsuit that would be perfect for work. The pants had a front-button band and zip-up placket. The jacket hung loose, but had darts in front and back, giving it a slightly fitted look. She had on a white lace camisole-type shell under the jacket.

A big smile played on Lana's face. She had to admit that she looked *fine* in this outfit. She decided to keep it on and surprise Tony when he got back.

The more she opened boxes and laid out clothes, the more she felt the room closing in on her. There was no reason she couldn't load these clothes in her car and take them to her house. She didn't have to wait until Tony could be with her. That was just silly.

With the decision made, she started making trips back and forth to her car. By the time she'd finished, her car was packed with boxes.

*Okay, that should do it*, Lana thought, putting a big box in her car. That's about all the car would hold, anyway.

Standing, her eyes voluntarily swept to the second floor window of the house next door. Was that a shadowy head that ducked back when she looked up? Had someone been watching her?

Mrs. Johnson had grown old and recently died in that house.

Had her spirit remained? Lana was sure nobody had bought the house. Her mom would have known if she had new neighbors.

A chill crept up Lana's spine as she headed back inside her mom's house, distinctly feeling that eyes followed her.

"Stop it!" she scolded herself aloud once she had the door closed. She was letting Tony's paranoia get to her. And she refused to do that. To prove her point, she grabbed her purse and went back to her car. She'd take these clothes to her house and hang them up. But she couldn't help glancing up at the window of the house next door. It seemed vacant—but was it?

**As she inserted the key into the door** of her house, a thought slid into her mind. Why weren't Ron's fingerprints on her door? If he had come over to her house as innocently as he claimed, then why would he have wiped his fingerprints off?

Either Ron was lying to her or someone else had been in her house. Suddenly her plan to come here alone didn't seem so smart. But she was here with a carload of clothes, so she planned to unload them.

Her jittery nerves had settled down completely by the time she'd unpacked and hung the last beautiful outfit in her closet. She looked around her little house lovingly. She resented that someone was making it impossible for her to get back to her normal life here.

A cool breeze gently ruffled the gauzy curtains beside her bed, reminding her that spring was her favorite time of the—

*She hadn't opened that window!*

The bedroom was small, so her bed was very close to the wall, making it hard to get to the window. But Lana squeezed beside the bed until she reached the window and pulled the curtains back. The window was barely open, almost as if it were left like that on purpose. The screen was in place, but the screens were easy to remove from the outside. If the police had checked the windows from the outside, they couldn't have seen that the window was barely open. And if they hadn't physically come behind the bed and pulled the curtains back, they wouldn't have noticed it either.

This window had to have been unlocked and opened from the inside. She always—*always* made sure her windows were locked.

She immediately called the police. Maybe there would be fingerprints on the inside of the window frame.

**Metro detective Jeff Collins** had just finished dusting for fingerprints when Tony came through the front door. "Lana?" he bellowed.

"In here!" she answered from the bedroom.

"What's going on?" he asked, looking from her to the detective. "And what were you doing here alone?" he asked Lana before either of them could answer him.

"Calm down, Tony. I'm okay." She proceeded to tell him about finding the open window.

"This is detective Jeff Collins," Lana added, indicating the man who was busily dusting for fingerprints.

He stopped long enough to acknowledge Tony, then said, "I got some good fingerprints off this frame. If we can find a match to these, we'll have something to go on. These criminals think they're so smart, but sooner or later they screw up. Just like this one. He was so careful to wipe his fingerprints off of everything except the inside of this window.

"This was a good catch, Miss Clarke. I'm sorry we missed this window when we were out here before. I'll let you know when we find the owner of these fingerprints."

Tony followed Detective Collins to his car, where they stood and talked for several minutes. When he came back inside, his face was dark with emotion.

"What's it going to take to convince you these people are dangerous?" he said. "I asked you to stay at your mom's until I got back, but you just had to come over here alone. What were you *thinking*?"

"I was *thinking*," Lana ground out, taking offense at Tony's tone with her, "that I won't be held emotionally or physically hostage by these creeps. I don't know what their goal is, *or* what their problem is, but if I keep hiding from them, then we'll never know. And I'll have to live in fear for the rest of my life. I'm *thinking* that the sooner I get back to my normal life and flush these fearmongers out, then we can get to the bottom of whatever they're trying to achieve."

Lana finished her heated declaration and started to move past Tony to go to the kitchen. She'd had enough. She would go back to work tomorrow and get her mind off all this. She was tired of thinking about it.

Tony's hand caught her arm and pulled her to him. "I'm sorry I pissed you off. But damn! You're even more beautiful when you're pissed! Will you forgive me? I shouldn't have used that tone on you. I'm just so worried about you. Lana, you have to remember that I've already lost loved ones that I suspect these 'fearmongers,' as you call them, had something to do with. I can't stand the thought of them taking another person I love from me."

Lana looked up into Tony's eyes. He was so sincere she had to believe him. Yet—love? Had he actually said that he loved her?

Before she could comment, his lips covered hers in a kiss that knocked all thoughts from her mind except the emotions that immediately boiled inside her. As he deepened the kiss, his arms pulled her hard against him, as if he was afraid she'd disappear from him at any moment.

"You taste so good," he whispered, trailing kisses down her neck and into the opening of her shirt. He kissed her cleavage and the rise of her breasts pushing up from her bra.

"I'm going crazy being around you all the time and not being able to touch you like this. I've almost slipped into your room at night after your mom went to sleep. Would you let me do that, Lana? Would you let me come to your room and make love to you?" His mouth claimed hers again, making an answer unnecessary.

Their breathing became one. Lana felt her entire body opening up for him. But her heart opened the most.

Tony satisfied everything she'd ever wanted or needed. Why not let him make love to her? She knew at this moment that he was the only man she'd ever loved. Maybe the only man she would ever love. He made her feel like a woman. She felt like she'd come home when she was in his arms.

And to let him know this she kissed him back as passionately as he was kissing her. She was about to lead him to her bed when the ringing of the doorbell broke into their consciousness.

Lana's nosy neighbor, Mrs. Andrews, stood just outside the door. Lana sometimes referred to her as the stand-alone neighborhood watch.

"Hi, Mrs. Andrews," Lana said, "Can I help you?"

"No. But I may be able to help you," she answered, pushing her way into the house. She nodded briefly to Tony before saying to Lana, "I've seen a lot of cop activity around here lately. I've also seen some other activity you might be interested in."

"What activity?" Tony asked.

"Can he be trusted?" Mrs. Andrews asked Lana.

"Yes. Absolutely."

"I was back yonder cleaning some trash out of my hedge bushes a few days ago, and I seen a skinny red-headed woman wearing bright red lipstick climbing in your window."

"Why didn't you call the police?" Lana asked.

"I was goin' to, but I got busy and forgot. Then you and the cops showed up later that day, so I figured you had it under control. But then I saw the cops back today, so I thought I might oughta tell you about the woman."

"I really appreciate it, Mrs. Andrews," Lana said. "I'm going to give you my cell phone number, and if you see anyone else except me messing around, please call me. And thank you for watching the neighborhood. You're a big help." Now Lana realized what a good thing a nosy neighbor can be sometimes.

Mrs. Andrews left, feeling very pumped up and important for her good deed.

"Well, it would appear as if our burglar is Maxie Simms," Tony said.

# *Chapter 11*

"**It seems Maxie has a pretty long record** with the police," Tony said after he got off his cell phone with Detective Collins. He'd called and asked the detective to run a check on Maxie after Mrs. Andrews left. "She's on probation for breaking and entering with the intent to rob a wealthy home six months ago."

"But why would she want to be in my house? I don't have any valuables."

"It's my guess that she's in with Dan somehow or other. I think she took your underwear as a mind game. They're trying to weird you out."

"So if she was in my house, I guess she wiped down all the door frames. I didn't think Ron would have deliberately wiped his fingerprints off. It didn't make any sense."

"Do you think he's in cahoots with them? Or is his relationship with Maxie totally innocent?"

"I think he's innocent," Lana answered. "But I think Maxie is using him. I just hope he doesn't fall in love with her before he finds out the truth. Do you think we should tell him?"

"I thought he was in love with you."

"Looking back over our past year together, I'm pretty sure Ron doesn't love me. He never tried to make love to me. We'd kiss occasionally, but it never got hot and heavy like—" Color flooded her face as she looked up at Tony.

"—like we do?" he finished for her.

"Yes."

"Then he doesn't love you like he should. But I don't think we need to tell him about Maxie. I'm afraid he'd let it slip if he knew."

"I agree. Especially if he considers himself enamored with her. At the same time, I'd hate to see him wind up in trouble with the law by association."

"Do you love him, Lana?"

"No. I care for him as a friend. But I can't see myself spending my life with him." Here she paused, wondering if she should speak freely, then decided to be completely honest with Tony. "Until recently, I didn't know what it meant to feel like a total woman. You awoke feelings in me that I didn't know I had. Now I know I'll never be content with anything less."

Tony pulled her close again and said, "You'll never have to be content with anything less as long as I'm around. But I've only started awakening those feelings for you. I want to make love to you, Lana. I want to hold you all night long. I want to kiss you all over, then start all over again."

Tony turned her on more just by talking to her than Ron ever had in his most passionate moment.

"But now isn't the time. I have to run to my office and sign some papers. Will you promise me that you'll go straight to your mom's? I'll be along in about an hour."

"Yes, I promise," Lana agreed. After finding her open window, she wasn't as gung-ho as she'd been a little earlier.

"Incidentally, you look fantastic in that outfit," Tony said.

"I wondered if you even noticed," Lana joked. "You flew in here yelling at me for being here and didn't seem to notice that I looked particularly hot today. And by the way, how did you know I was here?"

"I went back to your mom's because I'd forgotten a file I needed to work on. You weren't there and I saw that the boxes were missing from your room, so I deducted that you'd brought them over here. But trust me. I noticed how hot you look in that red outfit.

I just wish I could take time and let you know just how much I noticed."

Before he could kiss her again, she headed for the door. "Go to work, Tony. I don't want to be the one to cause your business to go under."

The chuckle that rumbled from his chest as he followed her out the door sent a wave of heat through Lana. Was there anything about this man that didn't cause her blood to heat up?

As she locked the door he swept her hair out of the way and kissed the side of her neck. "Tony! You know Mrs. Andrews is watching!"

"Well, she might as well get used to seeing me kiss you. The whole world might as well get used to seeing me kiss you!" he proclaimed. His arms swept the air, only to land around her shoulders and pull her to him, making good his promise as his lips claimed hers.

With much effort, Lana pushed away from him. "I'll see you at Mom's," she said, heading for her car.

"Another lonely night at Mom's," Tony called after her with a hurt sound in his voice.

Lana giggled as she sat down in her car.

Tony was the embodiment of manhood, as far as Lana was concerned. How had she gotten so lucky to find him? And would it last? Did he really love her? And was she really falling in love with him?

Her mind flashed back to the night he'd shown up at her mom's to discuss Jenny's wedding—Jenny's wedding!

They hadn't had a meeting to discuss the wedding in a while. She needed to talk with her mom about that. And she needed to talk with Jenny about the conversation they'd had the other night. She needed to let Jenny know all was forgiven and that she didn't hold any hard feelings toward her. Poor Jenny. Nobody had known how she'd suffered when Tommy died.

A loud clap of thunder and raindrops splattering on the car's windshield told her that a storm had approached without her paying attention. *Great!* she thought. She'd get her new outfit wet trying to get inside. She hadn't brought an umbrella with her, either.

Her mom's house sat on a corner lot, with a driveway to the front of the house from one street and a driveway to the back of the house from the side street. Lana decided to pull into the back of the house and go in through the patio. That would put her closer to shelter when she got out of the car. Too bad her parents had never actually built that garage they'd always wanted.

By the time she got out of the car the rain was coming down in sheets. Maybe she could get inside before the thunder and lightning got worse.

She'd just made it inside when she heard the phone ringing. She dashed to the living room, where the closest phone was. Checking the caller ID, she saw it was her mom's cell phone, so she answered.

"Thank goodness you're home! I've called five times and didn't get an answer. I was beginning to worry about you! I tried your cell phone, but didn't get an answer."

"I'm fine, Mom. You and Tony are starting to sound alike. I carried some of the clothes over to my house," Lana said. She wouldn't tell her mom about the open window just yet. "My cell phone was in my purse, but I didn't hear it ring."

"Well, we're just concerned about you. I'm in the grocery store. Is there anything you can think of that you'd like?"

"No. Nothing comes to mind, but thanks for asking."

As they signed off the call, a red spark of light in the upstairs window of the house next door caught Lana's attention. The spark glowed brightly for a few seconds, then lowered a couple of feet and dangled in the air. After a few moments, it lifted back up, glowed brightly, then lowered.

Someone was smoking a cigarette, apparently while looking out the window toward her mom's house. Someone was watching this house.

Her feeling of being watched that morning was real. And it wasn't a ghost. This was a real person, smoking a real cigarette. Apparently since she'd come in the back door they hadn't seen her car drive up. And since she hadn't turned any lights on, they didn't know anyone was home.

Lana lowered herself into a chair where she was sure they couldn't see her when the lightning flashed. She'd just watch them back. Maybe she could catch a glimpse of whoever it was during one of the sharp flashes of lightning.

The storm seemed to have stalled over the area. Loud crashes of thunder shook the house. If the storm clouds hadn't caused it to be so dark, she'd never have noticed the cigarette this time of day.

A particularly long display of lightning flashed across the sky, illuminating the window just in time for Lana to see a man's silhouette facing the window. Just then a second man's silhouette appeared, slapped the cigarette from the hand of the first, and shoved him out of view of the window.

So there were at least two people watching the house. Real fear crept up Lana's spine. Not for herself, but for her mom. Lana hated the fact that she and Tony had brought danger this close to her mom.

Well, she'd fix that. She'd go home tomorrow. And she'd make sure the people watching knew what she was doing. She'd make a big deal of the fact when she loaded her car. She might even stage a fight with her mom in the front yard, where they could hear her.

But she'd have to tell her mom and Tony when they got home. She couldn't let her mom be ignorant of what was going on.

Damn! She was tired of this! She had the urge to march across the street right now and accost those jerks. Her next impulse was to call the cops and tell them, but a little voice told her to wait and talk with Tony first.

In the meantime, she'd just sit here in the dark and wait for her mom to get home. If she turned on lights now, they'd know she came in the back way and might suspect that she'd seen them. Maybe she'd see something else while she watched.

After what seemed like hours, but was only thirty minutes, she heard her mom pull up in the driveway. She hurried to the kitchen so nobody would see her when Alma turned on the lights in the living room.

"Mom, I'm in the kitchen," she called as soon as she heard the front door open.

"What are you doing in the dark?" Alma asked, setting a sack of groceries down long enough to stand an umbrella in the corner before heading to the kitchen with the groceries.

Lana took the sack and put it on the counter. "I'd just come in when you called, so I hadn't taken time to turn on the lights. As I hung up the phone, I saw something in the window of the house next door. It turned out to be someone smoking a cigarette."

"What?" Alma said, turning to go look.

"No, Mom! Don't let them see you looking! We can't let them know we're suspicious. I'm going to tell Tony as soon as he gets here, and see if we should notify the cops or not."

"Well of course we should!" There was no question in Alma's mind.

"Let's see what Tony says, okay?" Lana insisted. "Are there more groceries?"

"No, this is all."

They quickly threw together some spaghetti, garlic bread and a salad and had it ready by the time they heard the front door opening.

"Tony, is that you?" Lana called.

"No, it's Hank and me," Jenny answered.

Lana's first reaction was dread, knowing that she'd have to face Jenny's tongue. Then she remembered their last conversation. But she couldn't help but wonder if Jenny would make some comment.

"Lana! You look beautiful," Jenny said, coming to give her a big hug. "I love the new look! Is that a new outfit?"

In all the excitement, Lana had forgotten she had on the new pantsuit. "Thank you. Yes, this is off of Tony's sale rack."

"You do look nice," Hank agreed.

"Have you two had dinner?" Alma asked.

"We ate before we came over," Jenny said. "But we'll sit and have coffee and watch you eat, if that's okay."

"Sure. And I'm sure you have room for some angel food cake and ice cream," Alma said.

"Is Tony coming?" Jenny asked.

"Yes, but I'm not sure when. I don't think we should wait on him," Lana said.

"Why don't you call him and see how soon he'll be here?" Alma said. "I hate to start if he's almost here."

Lana was about to push his number on her speed dial when she heard a knock on the front door. She went to check, and it was him.

"You have a key," she said, opening the door. "You don't need to knock."

"I know, but I was hoping you'd come to the door."

They were alone in the foyer, so he wrapped his arms around her and kissed her. "I've missed you," he whispered against her lips.

"I've missed you too," she giggled, feeling like a teenager. They'd only been apart a few hours.

"Now that's a nice welcome home," Alma spoke from behind them.

They jumped apart like two guilty kids.

"Oh, give me a break!" Alma said. "I've already said that I know something is going on between you two. In fact, you probably sneak to each other's beds during the night."

"Mom!" Lana couldn't believe what her mom had said.

Tony caught Alma in a bear hug and twirled her around the room. "I knew you weren't a fuddy-duddy like Lana seems to think," he said, planting a kiss on her cheek.

"Well, I'd prefer not to know it if you're playing hanky-panky in my house before you're married, but, at the same time I'm not dead yet, either."

After "hellos" were said all around and they were all sitting at the table, Jenny said, "Hank and I have an announcement."

All heads turned to her and waited.

"We're setting the wedding date up two months. It's going to be in June instead of August."

"Why?" Alma asked, looking panicky.

"At the rate people around here are gaining weight, nobody

will fit into her dress if we don't change the date," Jenny answered, looking at Hank.

Lana's heart nose-dived. She'd hoped so much that Jenny had truly changed her attitude. She stared at her plate for a few seconds before looking back at Jenny, who was smiling broadly at her.

"Not you, darling sister. Me. I'm two months pregnant!"

"What?" Alma, Tony and Lana chorused.

"Can you believe it?" Hank said. His grin couldn't have been bigger. Lana knew he'd seemed more animated today, and now she knew why.

Their joy was total. They couldn't have been happier, it seemed. "So Grandma, you might as well start deciding what you want to be called," Jenny kidded Alma.

"That's right! I'm going to be a grandmother! Oh, sweetheart, I'm so happy for you. But I can't help but wish you'd had a few months of wedded bliss before a baby came along."

"Well, Mom, it's not like Hank and I haven't had some time together," Jenny pointed out sheepishly.

"That's true. I keep forgetting that times have changed since your dad and I got married. So this means we'll have a wedding next month?"

"I'm afraid so, Mom," Jenny said. "I'm sorry for the inconvenience. I have to admit, we were a little nonchalant about birth control. But we wanted to start a family soon after we got married, anyway, so we're really happy about this.

"But we don't have to think about the wedding tonight. Hank and I want to put our heads together in the next few days and downsize the wedding plans some. That way it won't be so stressful on all of us."

Jenny turned to Lana with a very serious look on her face. "I've given this a lot of thought, Lana. I know that this baby could inherit the family fat gene, so I want you to be its godmother. I would want that anyway, but if I have a child that has a tendency to be a little butterball, I'll need a lot of help to make sure I do things right." Tears puddled in her eyes as she spoke.

"You got it, sis!" Lana agreed, going to Jenny and hugging

her. "With a mom like you and a grandma like Mom and an aunt like me, this child may wind up being the president of the United States!"

"And that's not saying anything about the magnificent men in its life," Hank jumped in.

"That's right," Tony said. "If it's a boy, you and I are going to have to work overtime to counteract all the estrogen that will surround the poor kid."

Everyone had a good laugh, but Lana's heart did a cartwheel. It sounded like Tony had plans to remain a part of the family.

**After Jenny and Hank were gone,** Lana turned to Tony. "We have to talk," she said.

"Now, I know you're not pregnant, but this sounds serious!" he tried to kid.

While Alma, Tony and she had another cup of coffee, Lana explained about the activity she'd seen in the house next door. "So for that reason, I'm going home tomorrow. I won't put Mom in this kind of danger."

"It's too late. We've already established that she's in danger, and this only proves it. I don't think your leaving will change that, now," Tony said.

# Chapter 12

**"The first night I stayed here** I thought something strange was going on next door," Tony told Lana and Alma. "I've had Tom checking it out, and he just found out today that it's some of Dan's buddies. For that reason I want all of us to go to my house until this mess is settled. My house and property are fenced-in and guarded, so we won't have to worry about anyone getting in or spying on us.

"What I'd like for each of us to do is just casually get in our cars tomorrow and drive away at different times. We can have a designated meeting time and spot and I can lead you to my house. That way we don't take a chance of them trying to follow us."

"I appreciate the offer, Tony," Alma said, "but I'm not leaving my home. I have a wedding to coordinate, and now I have one month to do it. I can't do that if I'm hiding out at your house. I'm sorry, but these buffoons are just going to have to watch me come and go at my own leisure." Lana saw the flash of fire in Alma's eyes that only appeared when she was dead serious and dug in.

"There is a very strong stubborn gene in this family," Tony said, shaking his head in part amusement and part frustration. "I'm really sorry your family is in danger just by association with me. I didn't know this would happen, or I would never have come here. But I did, and it did. Now, I could storm over to that house and tell those guys that we're on to them, but I spoke with the police yesterday, and they think Dan and his sidekicks are into something deep. Something other than a jealous lost-love situation. For that reason they want us to keep a low profile until we can find out what's going down. So if you refuse to leave this house, I'll just have to hire a bodyguard for you."

His look challenged Alma to argue with him, but she did. "I don't need a bodyguard. It's not me they're after. You just make sure my daughter stays safe, and everything will be okay."

"Trust me, Lana will be safe—if she'll listen to me. At this point, I don't think either of you are listening very well. Lana, please. If Alma insists on staying here, then please agree to stay here until after the wedding. You, Alma and Jenny will be spending a lot of time together finalizing the arrangements, so you might as well be here, rather than your house."

It did make sense when he put it that way, so Lana agreed. "Okay, but as soon as the wedding is over, I'm going home and back to my job. Carmen is going to get tired of hiring temps to cover for me."

"Carmen isn't having to deal with temps," Tony said. "I have a friend who's filling in for you while you're away."

*Of course*, Lana thought. Tony, the best man for everything. That's what Hank had said. And Tom had said the same thing. So far, they both seemed to be right.

**As Alma, Tony and Lana were having breakfast** the next morning, a firm knock sounded on the front door.

"Who on earth can that be at nine o'clock in the morning?" Alma wondered.

"I'll get it," Tony said.

The two women heard him talking with another man for a few minutes, then Tony came into the kitchen leading a tall, well-built man in jeans and a long-sleeved work shirt. He looked to be in his fifties, with pepper-gray hair, but his mustache and eyebrows were jet black. Twinkling blue eyes seemed to blaze from beneath the dark eyebrows.

Handsome. Authoritative. Reliable. All these words flashed

through Lana's mind as she looked at the man.

"Ladies, this is Jim," Tony said. "He's the new landscaper."

"For who?" Alma asked.

"For you," Tony answered. "Actually, he's a private detective. His hobby is landscaping, so he's perfect to hang out here. If it's okay with you, Alma, he'll plant some flowers, keep the yard groomed, etc., while he keeps an eye out for you ladies."

"What if it's not okay with me?" Alma asked, almost glaring at Tony. "You could have at least asked me before you brought a stranger into my house and announced that he was going to redo my yard. Maybe I like things just the damn way they are!"

"Mom!" Lana scolded. Her mom seldom used swear words. Normally Alma was the epitome of Southern grace, even if she was against something.

"Lana, your father planted every flower and shrub in that yard. He designed the layout. It was his cherished baby." Tears puddled in her eyes as she finished.

"I understand." The voice was strong, yet one of the kindest voices Lana had ever heard. "My late wife was our gardener while she was alive. I only started dabbling with landscaping after she died because I wanted to keep our yard looking exactly like she left it. It made me feel as if she was still there." Jim spoke directly into Alma's eyes, letting her know that he completely understood how she felt. "How about if I just trim the hedges, keep the grass cut and replace any flowers that aren't doing well? I promise not to touch anything that you tell me to keep my hands off of."

For some reason the last statement had a double meaning to Lana as she watched the look this newcomer was giving her mom.

"I'm sorry. Where are my manners?" Alma's tone had abruptly changed. "Please sit down and have coffee with us, and we'll talk about this."

Tony winked at Lana when she glanced at him. They had suddenly become nonexistent to Jim and Alma, who were rapidly into a deep discussion about plants and flowers.

"Maybe I could build you a couple of flower boxes for the front windows," Jim suggested.

"Oh! I've always wanted flower boxes," Alma exclaimed, clasping her hands together. "Howard was going to build me some, but just never got around to it."

Lana watched in amazement. She'd never seen her mom react to a man like this. She was almost acting like a teenager! This could really get interesting.

"Okay, I've got to run to the office for awhile, so I'll leave you to work this all out," Tony said. "The plans are that Jim will stay here until I get back for the night. That way you'll never be alone, okay?"

"Sure, Tony, and thanks," Alma said, taking her attention from Jim just long enough to answer.

Lana followed Tony to the door as he was leaving. "I hope you know what you're doing, Mr. Angelino. Did you provide a body guard or a love interest?"

"The love interest thing wasn't intended. Honest. I wanted Jim because he can pull off the landscaper look and actions so perfectly. But man! Did you feel the sparks fly between them?" A grin creased his face.

"What if Mom does become interested in him? Is he okay for her?"

"Jim Sinclair is a rock. He was a policeman until his wife got sick with cancer. He took time off to be with her. Then after she died, he kind of went into shock for a couple of years. He didn't work at anything. Finally he started to get his life back together, but decided he'd rather be a detective, so he started his own business. I'd trust my life with him. He's a good man. An honorable man.

"Now that I don't have to worry about your mom, how about you? Are you going to cooperate and stay safe, or am I going to have to handcuff you to myself just to keep an eye on you? Hmm," he said, stepping close and taking her in his arms. "That doesn't sound like a bad idea, after all. I'd love to be handcuffed to you." His lips were gentle as he backed her against the wall, deepening the kiss.

"Should we use the back door to go outside?" Alma asked from behind them. "We're going to the nursery to look at plants."

"Alma, you just keep interrupting my love life," Tony said, grinning, but not releasing Lana. They moved over to let the other couple pass, then Tony pulled Lana back to him.

"I thought you were going to the office," Lana whispered after he ended another long, probing kiss.

"I'd rather take you to your room and make slow, easy love to you." His voice was rough with emotion. "I think the handcuff thing set me off!" His smile was mischievous. "But, yes, I guess I do need to go. Be safe, my love," he said, quickly kissing her again and leaving.

Lana looked around the empty house and wondered what she was going to do to pass time. She hated this! Hated being a prisoner in her mom's house. But there wasn't much she could do about it at this point. She'd promised Tony.

Well, she might as well make herself useful and clean the house. She knew her mom would appreciate it. So she headed upstairs to slip into some jeans and a T-shirt.

She pulled on a pair of jeans and felt the snugness as they crept up her thighs. They weren't too tight yet, but well on the way.

The old familiar fat-panic attack slammed into her like a bolt of lightning. This was her last group of fat clothes, and she was about to outgrow them! This is where she usually came to a screeching stop and started the latest diet craze.

Most of the time the dieting consisted of skipping meals and basically starving until she felt the weight start to melt off her. How much bigger would she get if she kept going? The fear—that crippling fear of the unknown gripped her.

How fat would she get? Did she have a setpoint, a natural weight, and, if so, what was it? Would she be able to deal with her genetically programmed self? Would Tony want a wife the size she could become?

Without realizing it, she'd sat down on the side of her bed and was now clutching the mauve comforter with both hands.

"Stop it!" she admonished herself when she realized she was becoming agitated. "Just stop it. This is your decision," she continued her personal pep talk, "and you're sticking with it."

She stood and pulled on the T-shirt that she'd planned to wear. It, too, was very snug. She'd noticed that her bras were becoming too small, and the tight knit shirt revealed just how the bra was cutting across the top of her breasts, pushing everything it couldn't contain over the top. Oh, well. Nobody was going to see her while she cleaned house, anyway, so it didn't matter.

Slowly the panic attack lifted and she started feeling better. She put one of her mom's ZZ Top CDs in the player and pumped it up so she could hear it throughout the house. She checked the doors to make sure they were locked, since she wouldn't be able to hear anyone if they tried to break in.

She'd cleaned the kitchen, both bathrooms, and was vacuuming her room when she got the distinct feeling of being watched. She casually glanced at the door and screamed.

"It's okay, baby!" Tony said, rushing to her. "I came in and had just located you when you looked around. I didn't know how to get your attention without startling you."

She cut the vacuum off and tried to control her nerves. The problem wasn't that he'd startled her. The problem was that he was seeing her in these clothes that were too tight. But it was too late.

And she was trying to figure out the gleam in his eyes.

"You're one hell of a sexy cleaning lady, I can tell you that," he said, tracing the outline of the cleavage that showed through the T-shirt.

"Tony—"

"What?"

"What are you doing?" she asked as he pulled her to him.

"I'm feeling you up," he answered, as one of his hands cupped a breast.

"Tony!" Heat shot through her instantly.

"I said 'what?'" he answered, slipping his hand under the T-shirt to get a better feel. "I really like this look," he said, just before he captured her lips in his.

The kiss combined with his hand working its magic aroused Lana to the point of no return.

He eased her down onto the bed and lay back with her, while never losing contact with her lips. Her head rested in the crook of his arm while his other hand continued to explore the treasures he'd wanted to explore again ever since bathing her in the Bahamas.

She pulled him close. Oh! He felt so good. It felt so good to be with him like this.

"This is heaven," he whispered, raising the shirt enough to allow his kisses to gently cover her ribcage before coming back to her lips.

She felt his hands fumbling with the snap on her jeans and almost panicked. "Tony, no." She whimpered, but didn't try to stop him.

"I just want to touch you there. I want to see if I affect you the way you affect me," he said, slowly sliding his hand downward, seeking the core of her being. When his fingers touched their goal, Lana's body shook with emotion.

"Tony!" she tried to protest.

"Shhh. Relax and let me love you." He kissed her breasts through the lace of her bra.

"Anybody home?" Alma's voice called from the front of the house at the same time the music was shut off.

"Damn!" Tony said, quickly rising from the bed.

"In my room, Mom," Lana called, madly adjusting her clothes and straightening the bed.

"Come on in the kitchen. I have a surprise," Alma called. "Is Tony in his room?"

"No, he's just come in here and scared me to death," Lana answered, almost laughing out loud as Tony tried to adjust himself to hide the effect of their brief lovemaking.

"I'll go ahead while you contain yourself," she giggled, and headed for the door.

"Tease," he accused her, reaching for one more touch before she escaped and headed for the kitchen.

Lana had forgotten that Jim might come in with her mom, so she was surprised to see him relaxing in a dining room chair with a glass of iced tea.

"You've been cleaning," Alma stated. "I love it when you do that. You know I don't care for housework at all. I'd rather be doing just about anything else."

"My pleasure, Mom. I had to do something to pass the time while I was held prisoner in the house. But I meant to change out of these old clothes before everyone got back home. I'm afraid I've about outgrown all my fat clothes. It's a good thing Tony took me shopping."

"You look great in those clothes," Alma assured her. "In fact, you look really sexy. Maybe you should go and change before Tony sees you. You could cause a man a heart attack in that tight shirt."

"Mom!" Lana said, casting a glance at Jim.

"Lana, could you come here, please?" Tony called from the living room.

He was standing with the front door open when she got to him. "My, um—body doesn't seem to be cooperating yet, so I can't come in the kitchen. I keep thinking of how you look in that outfit, so I'm going outside to walk this off."

All he heard was her peal of laughter as he closed the door behind him.

She relished the surge of power that charged through her body. She felt exhilarated that she had that much effect on him.

"Tony's checking something in his car," Lana explained to her mom and Jim. "He'll be back in soon. What's the surprise?"

# Chapter 13

**Just then Jenny, Hank and Tony** came into the kitchen. "This is the surprise," Alma said, pointing at Jenny and Hank.

At Lana's blank look Jenny held up her left hand, which was weighted down with a huge diamond in the middle of a wide gold band. "We're married," Jenny announced, giving Hank a big hug.

"What?" Lana and Tony exclaimed at the same time.

"Hank's parents threw such a hissy fit over me being pregnant and showing at the wedding, afraid that we would embarrass them and all their hoity-toity friends, that we just eloped!"

"We decided this would be the most simple solution, in the long run," Hank said, then turned to Alma. "I want to apologize to you in person for spoiling the pleasure of helping your daughter plan her wedding. I know that's important to moms."

"Well, some moms, I guess, but my main concern is that you two are happy. And if this is what makes you happy, then I'm happy," Alma said, hugging both of them. "Besides, I still have another daughter I can plan a wedding for." She gave Tony a wicked wink.

"Don't even think about it, Mom!" Lana said.

"Now, Lana, don't be so quick to stop your mom's fantasies," Tony countered.

Ignoring the teasing light in Tony's eyes, Lana asked Alma, "So, Mom, how did you know that they'd eloped?"

"We bumped into them at the grocery store. They were trying

to be so cool, calm and collected. But it didn't take me long to spot the rock on Jenny's hand."

"Plus, under the circumstances, it was getting harder and harder to concentrate and plan a wedding," Hank spoke up. "Jenny's worried about Alma and Lana, and has her mind on a baby, now, so it just made more sense to do it this way."

As they talked, Alma set out makings for sandwiches and put paper plates and utensils on the table for everyone. She'd made sure that Jim was sitting next to her, Lana noticed. Jenny noticed, too, and gave Lana a questioning look.

"Jenny, would you like to come with me while I change clothes? I don't think I can eat with these tight jeans on," she said. That would give her an excuse to get out of these clothes and to explain to Jenny that Jim was there to help look after them in Tony's absence.

"He's a hunk!" Jenny said. "Do you think Mom has a thing for him?"

"I think the 'thing' is mutual," Lana said, slipping into a pair of navy slacks and a red knit sweater. The slacks fit as if they'd been tailored for her. She put on a pair of drop pearl earrings and a pearl and gold beaded necklace.

"You look really good, Lana," Jenny said. "I'm so sorry for hurting you all those times."

"I know you are. And now that I know why, I can even understand your motives. Don't think another thing about it, Jenny. I love you too much to let words come between us. Now come on. Let's go get a sandwich. You have a baby to feed, and I have a growing body to feed!"

Laughing, arm in arm, the two sisters joined the others in the dining room.

"Wow!" Alma said. "I really like that outfit, too. Tony, you did a great job picking out those clothes."

"Hmm. I think I like the other outfit better," Tony said, giving Lana a wicked grin.

"Yeah, you would," she countered. "I'm beginning to believe you're just a dirty old man."

"Come over here and sit beside me and I'll show you 'old,'" he answered, pulling out the chair beside him.

"You two behave, now," Alma scolded, and started passing around the sandwich makings.

The next day was a repeat of the day before. Alma and Jim left to check out more options for the yard, Tony went back to his office, and Lana wound up at home alone.

She was rebelling at the idea when the phone rang. "Lana?" Ron's voice asked.

"Hi, Ron. Yes, it's me."

"I need to talk with you. Will you have lunch with me today?"

"Sure," she answered. Why not? The thought of being housebound all day was not appealing to her at all. She left her mom a note explaining where she was going and that she'd be back in a couple of hours. She'd be back before Tony even knew she was gone, so she decided not to call and let him know. If she drove straight to meet Ron, then straight home, no harm could come to her.

She parked in front of Kookie's, a small, out-of-the-way hamburger joint that Ron had requested. That seemed a little strange to Lana, and she thought Ron's voice had sounded odd when he called. His car was already in the parking lot, so she went inside.

Ron was standing just inside the door and greeted Lana with his typical kiss on the cheek when she entered. "I'm sorry about this little place," he said. "But I didn't want to take a chance of anyone seeing us."

They bought their food, then sat down at a booth. Lana's glance landed on a large black man seated at the other end of the room. Tom Hoover. Their eyes met, but he shook his head "no," warning her not to speak to him. She lowered her eyes quickly and looked at the food on her plate.

Tom Hoover. Warmth spread through her. She wouldn't be sitting here right now if not for him. But why was he here? Obviously he'd gotten here before she and Ron. He already had food on his plate. She would love to go to him, wrap her arms around him and thank him for risking his life to save her, but she knew she'd endanger him if she did, so she sat and tried to ignore the fact that he was there.

Tony must have warned him to keep a closer eye on her. But how did Tom know she was coming here? Maybe he was following Ron. That made more sense. Tony must have told him to keep an eye on Ron.

"Lana? Is your food okay? Why are you looking at it like that?"

"Oh! It looks really good for a small place like this. I'm just surprised, I guess." She quickly covered her surprise at seeing Tom, then continued, "What's the mystery, Ron? Why wouldn't you want anyone to see us? We used to be seen together quite a lot."

"Lana, I've got to tell you something that has me really shaken up." Lana noticed his hands slightly shaking while he talked.

"What, Ron? What is it?"

"You know that Maxie works at Hanzel's Corporation, with me. Our email addresses are really close to being the same because of our names. My email address is rs@hanzelcorp.com and hers is rxs@hanzelcorp.com. Well, someone meant to send her an email, but left the 'x' off, and I got it. All the message said was *Information at doingthedeed.com.* At that point I still thought the email was for me, so out of curiosity I clicked on the website, and Lana, something weird is going on! Apparently, the website is a secret site that's used to pass information between people who are in on some kind of crooked scheme."

Lana waited until the waitress set their food down, then asked, "What kind of scheme? And why is this so upsetting?"

"I didn't take time to check it out because I didn't want to get caught, but yours and Tony's names were mentioned several times on the site."

"What?"

"Lana, the terms used sounded like death threats to you. Baby, I'm so scared for you. What have you gotten yourself into?"

"Okay, Ron. It's time you knew what's been happening. But I

think we need to go for a long ride to discuss this. I don't want to sit here and talk about it."

After they finished their hamburgers, they got in Ron's Mercedes. While he drove, Lana told him everything that had happened. About the incident in the Bahamas. Their suspicion of Maxie's involvement with Dan. That someone was spying on them from the house next door to her mom's.

"But you can't let anyone know about this, Ron," she finished. "You have to keep doing exactly what you've been doing with Maxie. Don't let her get suspicious of you. And if you hear of anything else, please let me know."

By now they were back at Kookie's.

"Are you going to be okay? I've been worried sick about you since I saw that website."

"I'm going to be fine. You just take care of yourself and don't get caught. Did you delete that email?"

"Yes. I deleted it, then deleted it from the trash folder, then deleted it from the internal hard drive. I can't take the chance of that being on my computer at work."

"Hmm. I wonder if Maxie knows how to delete her emails from the hard drive? If she doesn't, you could probably find out a lot of information from them," Lana said.

"That's a good idea! I stay after work a lot of days, so I'll try to find a time to check her computer."

"Be careful, Ron. These are dangerous people. I don't want you to get hurt."

"Baby, I've missed you," he said.

Before Lana could answer him, her cell phone rang. "Where the hell are you?" Tony's irate voice asked from the other end.

Lana glanced at her watch and realized that four hours had passed since she'd left her mom's house.

"I'm on my way home right now. I'll be there in twenty minutes." She hung up and didn't give him time to answer.

"Ron, I really have to go. They're worried about me. I wasn't supposed to leave the house today."

As Ron drove away with a worried look on his face, Lana hoped he could keep his cool in the new situation that had developed.

As soon as she pulled into the driveway Tony rushed out the front door, with Alma and Jim on his heels.

"We were worried sick about you!" he exclaimed, snatching her close in an almost angry embrace.

"Whoa! What's going on?" Lana asked, stepping back from him.

"Come inside and we'll explain," Alma said, putting her arm around Lana's shoulders and walking with her.

Once inside, Lana turned to the three people. "I had lunch with Ron, and it went longer than I expected. But Mom, I left you a note."

"What note? There wasn't a note. Lana, someone broke in the house. When I came home and you were gone, I panicked. I was about to call the police when Tony got here, and he had the common sense to call your cell phone. I didn't even think about that. I just panicked."

"Where did you leave the note?" Tony asked.

"Beside the coffeemaker. I know the first thing Mom does when she gets home is make coffee, so that's where I always leave my notes."

Tony left the living room, where they'd stopped, and went to the kitchen.

"How did they break in?" Lana directed her question to Jim.

"They pried open the sliding glass door. It won't be hard to fix, and I'll do that before I go home."

"Did they take anything?"

"Not that I can tell," Alma said.

"There is no note." Tony's voice preceded him into the room. "I looked everywhere it could have fallen, but it's just not there. Why did you leave the house?" he asked Lana.

"Ron called and wanted me to have lunch with him. He sounded strange, so I went. And don't lecture me. I know I'm supposed to be hiding out, but I don't always do what I'm supposed to do, okay?" She realized as she spoke that her voice was shaking. The day was catching up with her.

Tony didn't lecture. Instead he came and wrapped her in his arms and held her close. It felt wonderful to rest her head on his shoulder for just a moment. Safe and protected.

"The police are here," Jim said. "We need to give them a report."

Detective Collins followed two policemen into the house. "Man, I think trouble is following you around," he said, shaking hands with Tony. "I couldn't believe it when you called and said you'd had another break-in, at a different house."

Then he discovered Jim and his face broke into a huge grin, "Jim Sinclair! You old dog, what're you doing here?"

Tony, Jim and Detective Collins huddled and discussed why Jim was "hanging around." The policemen dusted for fingerprints, took down the report, and left.

Detective Collins was still talking with Tony and Jim. Alma had made a fresh pot of coffee, and the three guys were huddled around the dining room table discussing the case.

Well, she might as well get this over with, Lana decided. "I need to join you guys when you reach a place you can be interrupted," she said.

Tony immediately pulled out a chair beside him and motioned for her to sit. "Mom, you need to hear this, too," Lana said, sitting down beside Tony.

Then she proceeded to tell them everything Ron had told her.

Tony went to his room and got his laptop computer and looked up the website. "This is some incriminating stuff, Collins," he said. "But there are no names on it except mine and Lana's. Is there any way this site can be searched? Can emails from the site be traced?"

"I'm not sure, but we have a computer tech at the office. I'll ask him."

"Ron deleted the emails from his computer, but he doesn't know if Maxie deleted hers or not. He's going to check her computer one day after she leaves work," Lana said.

"Tell him to keep us informed of anything he finds, and not to destroy any evidence. In fact, tell him to forward them to me at my office. Here's my card with the email address on it. And tell him to make sure he deletes the forwarded emails from her "sent" box.

"I know I don't have to stress to you folks to be careful, but this case is becoming stranger all the while. It's a hard case because there doesn't seem to be any rhyme or reason to it. Why is this guy so determined to harass you?" Detective Collins literally scratched his head in confusion.

"Tony, is Jeff aware of what happened to your first wife?" Jim asked.

"What about her?" Detective Collins quickly responded.

"She and my son died in a suspicious fire. It was ruled an accident, but I was never convinced. I couldn't persuade anyone to open the case to possible foul play. It seemed to be a cut-and-dried case in everyone's eyes but mine."

"Tell me about it," Detective Collins said.

"Okay, but could we do this somewhere else? These folks have already heard the story, so I'm sure they don't want to sit through it again."

"Actually, we do," Alma cut in. "We're practically family now, Tony. Don't close us out."

So Tony told the story about his wife dying in what was considered to be a smoking accident. He told about Dan Smith's obsession with Mary.

When he'd finished, Detective Collins asked, "So do you think Dan Smith is capable of murder?"

"I do," Lana spoke quietly. "I saw it in his eyes when he thought he was going to kill me. I've never seen colder, harder eyes. Yes, he is capable of murder."

"Okay. Tomorrow I'm going to pull all the files on your wife's death. Maybe I can find something that was overlooked."

"He told me he'd made a pact with the devil that Anthony Angelino would never find happiness because he stole his girl. That sounds like motive to me," Lana cut in.

"Wait a minute! What's she talking about?" Detective Collins questioned Tony.

"We told you that Dan had tried to leave her stranded in the ocean," Tony reminded him.

"I know that. I've recorded all that. But I don't remember this part of it. I don't think you told me this. But even if you did, all that's going on seems a little elaborate just to get vengeance on a rival for love."

"Not if you realized, after you'd destroyed the woman and her child, that the child was actually your son."

# Chapter 14

**The room had gone suddenly quiet.**

"Tony! What are you saying?" Lana asked.

"After Mary and I had been married for a while, Dan showed back up and started hanging around. I finally had a restraining order put on him so he couldn't come near Mary again.

"A few months after that, Mary informed me that she was three months pregnant. She wanted to get an abortion, but I adamantly refused. She hated being pregnant. And she almost hated Gino when he was born. She wouldn't have anything to do with him. I had to hire a sitter for him during the day, and I took care of him at night. When I traveled, I had to hire a sitter around the clock.

"I couldn't understand a mother who despised her child so much. Gino was a wonderful baby. I loved him instantly. So I insisted that Mary get counseling.

"She didn't want counseling, so she finally told me that Dan had raped her one night while I was out of town. She thought the baby was his. I argued that there was a better chance the baby was mine, but she just *knew* it was Dan's. So I finally gave in and had a DNA test done. Sure enough, Gino was not my baby. But by then I didn't care. I loved him as if he were my own.

"After I found Dan's class ring in Mary's car, I insisted that he be brought in for questioning. I'd explained to the arresting officer that I knew Dan had raped Mary, and out of stupidity I also told him that Gino was Dan's son. I never meant for Dan to find that out, but the young officer let it slip."

"What was Dan's reaction?" Jim asked.

"He went ballistic and started accusing me of killing them. I had already been cleared of any suspicion, and the fire had been deemed an accident.

"So I'm sure his vengeance against me is more than a lost love. It's a perceived lost love and a lost child."

"This is a strange case, to say the least," Detective Collins said. "I'm going back to the office with this new information. I'll get Thomas to see what he can come up with on this website, and I'll see what I can dig up on your case, Tony. In the meantime, you folks really need to be careful."

"So if nothing was taken, why did they break in?" Lana asked. She saw a look pass over Tony's face. "What, Tony? What aren't you telling me?"

"When I went to get my laptop, this note was on my bed." He opened the note and read, "*Don't be afraid, Tony. You're safe. You must live to suffer.*"

"When were you going to show this to me?" Collins asked.

"When you went to your car. I didn't really want to the women to know about it."

"Okay. That does it," Alma said. "We've got to stop this guy. He's going to hurt someone if we don't. I want him picked up tomorrow. I know he's going to hurt Lana. We've got to stop him!" Jim placed a comforting hand on her arm.

"We can't do that yet," Detective Collins said. "I want more on him. I want to see if we can get some incriminating information from this website, and I want to see what the emails say, if this Ron guy can find them. I want enough to put Dan Smith away for a long, long time."

"Then you make sure my daughter is safe! If she'd been here alone today, there's no telling what they would have done to her."

"Alma," Tony interrupted, "They knew everyone was gone. That's why they came in. They didn't want to hurt anyone today. In fact, I'm sure they have orders not to touch anyone yet. They're just trying to intimidate us at this point."

"If he knows I'm still alive, it looks like he'd be running scared," Lana said. "He told me who he was because he was so sure his plan would work. So he knows that you all know he tried to kill me."

"Dan seems to have a disconnect from reality," Tony said. "Somewhere along the way he decided that anything he wants is attainable and that nobody can stop him. So I don't think he's really worried about what we know. His main goal is to cause me pain. And he knows I'll suffer if he hurts you." Tony had placed an arm around Lana's shoulders while he talked. "Detective Collins, I agree with Alma. We have to stop this bastard before he gets to Lana. Take a few more days, but that's all. With Lana and Tom's testimony, we have enough on two counts of attempted murder to keep him in jail for awhile."

"Okay," Detective Collins said. "Let me get on this. I'll talk to you folks as soon as I find out anything."

**A few days later Lana stood at the kitchen window** and watched Alma and Jim working in the yard. Lana was amazed at how her mom had taken to Jim. And Jim was obviously smitten with Alma.

The two were trying to uproot an old stump. They weren't getting very far. Lana decided to slip into some jeans and see if they needed help.

In her room, she took a pair of jeans from the clothes Tony had brought her, fully expecting that by now she couldn't fit into them. She was pleasantly surprised when they slid up and fastened with no effort. She hadn't gained any weight in more than a week!

Maybe this was where she'd stop, she thought. But then she realized it didn't matter. Suddenly she realized that it *really* didn't matter anymore.

A jolt of freedom shot through her. She was learning to live fat-phobic free!

Glancing in the mirror, she also realized she liked the curves reflected back at her. Actually, she'd always liked the way she looked at this size. She felt "at home" at this size. But she'd always given in to peer pressure to be thin. Not anymore! Those days were gone forever.

Feeling freer than she could ever remember feeling, she bounded down the stairs to go help her mom and Jim. She opened the door to find her mom reaching for the knob.

"Oh! You startled me!" Alma said. "Jim and I are running over to his house to get a pulley to use on this stump. I was just coming to tell you."

"Well, I was heading out to try and help you. But I think a pulley would be a better idea."

Lana closed the door and locked it. She hated the vulnerable feeling that always came over her now when she was alone. Damn Dan Smith, anyway! She was so tired of having her life tampered with.

Just as she started to walk away from the door a loud pounding startled her. *What on earth?* She knew her mom wouldn't knock like that. Besides, she'd watched Alma and Jim drive away. She peeked cautiously through the window to find Ron standing outside.

"There's something going down tonight, Lana!" he said, not taking time to exchange greetings when she opened the door.

"What are you talking about?"

"Maxie called in sick today, so when everyone went to lunch I checked out her email. There's something happening tonight. You said to let you know. I didn't want to call from the office, so I drove over. Here, I printed out the email. Is Tony here? Do we need to call the cops?"

"Ron! Sit down and relax. Do you want something to drink?" Lana noticed his shaking hands.

"No, I'm fine. I'm just not used to playing detective. It gets the adrenalin going."

"Tell me about it. I'm not used to playing the victim, either," Lana said as she dialed Tony's cell phone.

She read the email to him over the phone. "Okay, this sounds like we're on to something," he agreed. "Let me call Detective Collins and I'll get back with you. I don't think we should all show up at Alma's. If the goons next door are watching they might suspect that we're on to them."

In a few minutes Tony called back and gave instructions for Ron to meet him and Detective Collins at the police station. "You stay there. There's no need for you to come down to the station," he told Lana.

Lana agreed that there was no need for her to be with them. She'd probably just get in the way. If the email was legitimate, one of the historic homes of Mobile would be broken into tonight.

She was too strung out to read a book or watch TV, so she did some laundry and straightened up the house a little. She'd just take the trash out, then start dinner.

Just as she started out the back door with the trash bag in her hands the house phone rang, so she set the bag down and answered. It was her mom saying that she and Jim were going out to eat and to a movie. They had decided to put the stump pulling off until the next day.

Lana didn't bother telling her mom about the latest development with Ron. Alma thought Tony would be home by now. So let her mom have a worry free evening with Jim.

But so much for fixing dinner. She had no idea when Tony would be home.

After getting off the phone with her mom, she plopped down on the living room sofa. Her mom sounded so happy. Was she falling in love with Jim? Or was she just happy to have someone to hang out with? And what if she did fall in love with him? That would change their entire family dynamics. The thought made Lana smile. What dynamics? Those had changed when her dad died. And now Jenny was married, and she, Lana, hoped to be married one day. Soon, if she were honest with herself. So why shouldn't Alma be happy?

Remembering the trash, Lana got up to finish her chore. As she dropped the bag into the dumpster and turned to go back inside, she saw a police car pulling slowly into the back driveway.

"Can I help you, Officer?" she asked when a tall lanky man got out of the car.

"Ms. Clarke? I need for you to go with me to your house. It

seems you've had another break-in."

"Oh, man!" Lana exclaimed. "What did they do this time?"

"Well, I think it's best you just come with me."

"I need to call Tony," she said.

"He's on his way over there."

"Okay. Let me get my purse and lock the doors. I'll be right back."

"We don't have time for all that, ma'am," the policeman said, taking Lana's arm and hurrying her to the passenger's side and opening the door. Detective Collins and Tony will be there by now, waiting on you."

As Lana buckled her seat belt, she realized she didn't have her cell phone, purse, or anything. "Officer, I really need to get my purse and cell phone," she said, reaching for the door handle.

"It's too late. We don't have time," he answered, and backed swiftly out of the driveway.

"Can't you tell me what they did?" Lana asked.

"You'll know as soon as we get there. I'm not supposed to tell you any more than that."

"What's your name?"

"Bob," he said.

All the mystery had Lana's nerves more on edge than usual. Why wouldn't he tell her what had happened? Had the damage been that great? What could someone have done that couldn't be repeated?

She thought she was going to explode with unanswered questions when they finally turned down her street and pulled into her driveway.

"There's nobody here! Where is everyone?" Suddenly she was suspicious.

"Just get out of the car and go into the house," the officer said.

"I can't."

"Why the hell not?"

Would a real officer talk to her like that? "Because I don't have a key. You wouldn't let me get my purse, and my keys are in my purse."

Suddenly she didn't think it was a good idea to tell him about the second back-up key that was taped under a branch of the cedar tree that grew at the corner of her house. She was becoming more and more suspicious of this Officer Bob. She'd just wait until someone else got there before she told anyone where the key was.

"Well, we'll just have to improvise," he said. "Come on."

Lana stayed in the car and the officer came around to the passenger side. When he opened her door, Lana found herself looking into the barrel of his pistol.

"Now you get out of this car and act very natural. The neighbors are used to seeing police cars here, and you with them. So I want this to look like just another investigation."

"Which, apparently, it isn't," Lana concluded.

She got out of the car and walked ahead of the person in uniform to the front door. Standing very close to the door, he used the butt of his pistol to break the glass panel, then reached in and turned the lock.

*Please be watching, Mrs. Andrews*, Lana silently beseeched her nosy neighbor. Her heart was pounding. She sensed that something very bad was going down, right here in her own home.

Bob took a glass from her kitchen cabinet and filled it with tap water. Then he took a package of white powder, sprinkled it into the water, and mixed it until the powder dissolved.

"Here, drink this," he said.

"I don't think so," Lana said, and shoved his hand away from her.

"Do you want to die?" he asked.

"Somehow I don't believe you'll be the one who kills me," she answered. "I think you're in cahoots with Dan Smith, and I think *he* probably wants the pleasure of doing me in. But just out of curiosity, are you a real cop? And, if so, why did you go bad?"

"You talk a lot for someone about to die, don't you?"

"Why not? If I'm going to die, I might as well get some answers."

"Well, you won't get them from me. Dan told me to watch

you, because you're cagey."

"So you do know Dan."

Realizing he'd said too much, he pushed the glass back at Lana. "I know your mom's at the Regal Cinema tonight with her bodyguard boyfriend. I know what movie she's watching and I know when it's over. And I know you don't want anything bad to happen to her. So you just be a good girl and take this sleeping powder. It won't hurt you. You'll just go to sleep like a newborn baby."

"Then what? Dan will come in and kill me? Maybe burn the house down like he burned down Tony's house?"

Bob's face turned a dark red. "I don't know anything about that. And I don't know what Dan plans to do. I'm just following my instructions."

Not doubting that her mom was in danger, Lana took the drink and touched her lips to the liquid. It was slightly bitter. Lana turned up her nose.

"All I have to do is make one phone call and the brake line on Jim's car will be cut while they're in the movie. Anything can happen when a person's brakes go out in busy traffic."

Hearing the threat, Lana took a sip of the polluted water. Bob smiled and turned to the sink to rinse out the plastic bag that had contained the powder. When his back was turned, Lana spit the water that she'd held in her mouth onto the floor.

What did it matter? Her house would be in ashes before morning, anyway. She glanced around her home and was overcome with sadness. Sadness that she probably wouldn't live through the night. Sadness that her mom and Jenny would have to mourn her death. Sadness that she'd never get to make love with Tony, much less live a long, happy life with him.

"Drink!" The sharp demand brought Lana back.

"I'm drinking. This stuff tastes like crap. I can't just swig it. I'll throw it up if I do."

"Just hurry up! I'm on a time schedule, and I'm already behind."

"Then why don't you leave and take care of your other business?"

"You *are* my business. I'm supposed to have you asleep by now."

"Too bad."

"Yes, I guess it's too bad for your mom and Jim. And Jim was such a good man. What a waste. I don't know anything about your mom, but I'm sure she's a good person, too. Too bad they'll be injured, maybe killed, in a car accident." He picked up the phone as if to call someone.

"All right! I'm drinking!" Lana tilted the glass up and pretended to drink the liquid. She did swallow some of it, but managed to hold the glass at an angle so that most of the water flowed out of the corner of her mouth that was away from Bob. Hopefully, she wasn't getting enough to make her go totally to sleep. Thank goodness she'd worn a white blouse today. Maybe he wouldn't notice that it was becoming soaked.

She handed him the glass and realized that she was already feeling the effects. The room seemed to tilt the slightest, so she sat down on her couch.

"No, not there. Come on back to your bedroom," he ordered, leading her to her bedroom, where he motioned toward her bed. "Go on, lie down!" Impatience edged his voice.

Lana's eyes were closed by the time her head touched the pillow.

# Chapter 15

**Lana vaguely heard the front door close.** Officer Bob was gone. But how long would it be until Dan got here? She had to fight off the fog and dizziness trying to engulf her. She *could not* allow herself to go to sleep.

But she had to pretend to be asleep. Even in her drugged state, Lana realized the only way she was going to catch Dan Smith in his attempt to kill her was to go along with his plan. She had no idea what that plan was or how long she could go along with it, but she had to try.

Maybe if she got up and ate something, the food would weaken the effect of the drugs. She tried to sit up, but the room spun out of control and she fell back onto her pillow. *So much for that plan*, she thought, closing her eyes against the spinning ceiling.

She was losing the battle to stay awake when she heard the back door opening. A shot of adrenalin blasted through her system, causing her eyes to fly open. She heard footsteps approaching her room.

She closed her eyes. Whoever this was had to believe she was asleep. Thankfully, the room was growing dim from the setting sun. Surely he wouldn't turn the lights on to do his dirty work.

"Well, hello, there, Sleeping Beauty." She recognized Dan Smith's voice as he approached her bed. "That mouth of yours isn't running so much this time, is it?"

He placed rough hands on her shoulders and shook her. "Just making sure you're asleep. You have an irritating way of not dying when you're supposed to. This time will be different, though."

He took a wad of cotton material and stuffed it into her mouth, and roughly applied a strip of tape across the lower part of her face. "Yep, you ain't talking much now, are you?"

He proceeded to go to the foot of her bed and tie her ankles together. She fought the panic that tried to rise inside her. Just knowing she couldn't run was far more frightening than she'd ever dreamed it would be.

"Now that should make it easier to roll you around. You're going to be harder than Mary was. She was a little thing, but you, on the other hand, are not so little. Maybe I should have brought some help with me."

By now the room was dark enough that Lana felt safe in opening her eyes just enough to peer through her eyelashes at him. He spread a white sheet over her body, then proceeded to roll her over on her left side, away from him.

"Damn! This isn't going to be easy. If I could get to the other side of the bed and pull you over, it'd be better. Who puts their bed that close to the wall anyway? Stupid bitch."

Lana had to remind herself to keep her body totally relaxed, as if she were in a drug-induced deep sleep. That wasn't easy when every fiber of her being wanted to stiffen up and resist. But she managed to stay limp as he rolled her back toward him.

He was rolling her up, mummy style, in the sheet. He took her right hand out and placed it over her head, leaving it out of the mummy wrapping.

After pulling and tugging the sheet under and around her, he rolled her back toward the window. As he rolled her over, Lana felt her free hand moving in a natural way that would take it past his head, so she used the chance and guided the hand so it managed to whack him across his cheek and ear.

"What the hell? Did you slap me, bitch?" He stopped his frantic movements and stared down at her. In spite of her dire situation it was all she could do to keep from laughing at the startled look on his face as he covered his ear.

Finally, convincing himself that she was still asleep, he went back to his job. After wrapping her to his satisfaction, he lowered her free arm so it hung over the side of the bed. He took a short strip that he'd torn off the sheet and tied her arm to the bed frame, making her arm hang at a sharp downward angle. After making sure the tie was secure, Dan went to the foot of the bed and tied her ankles to the bedpost.

He was covering all angles. Leaving no way for her to escape.

Dan took a pack of cigarettes from his bag. Taking a cigarette from the pack, he placed the remaining pack on the nightstand beside the bed. He turned his back to her and the window and lit the cigarette. After it was burning to his satisfaction, he placed the cigarette between her forefinger and middle finger, as if she were smoking it. To insure it didn't fall he tied a strip of the torn sheet around her fingers, below the cigarette, to hold them together.

Then he piled a stack of what looked like tissue paper directly under her hand. "Just like poor Mary. Went to sleep smoking and woke up dead! Except this time my son won't die with you. But again the mighty Anthony Angelino will know what it's like to lose someone he loves. Poor Tony." His maniacal laugh bounced off the walls of her room as he took the bag he'd brought his stuff in and left the house.

Now Lana knew how Mary Angelino had died. But would she live to tell it?

She raised her head enough to see the glowing cigarette between her fingers. The tilt of her hand gave the cigarette enough upward gravity to keep the fire burning. When the burning cigarette got short enough, it would ignite the strip of cotton sheet that Dan had tied her fingers together with, and allow the burning cigarette and the cotton strip to fall into the tissue paper on the floor. The tissue paper would instantly ignite and set her bed on fire. Then the entire house would go up in flames.

Lana figured she had approximately five to ten minutes to figure her way out of this. The effects of the sleeping powder had mostly worn off—probably because of her pounding heart and adrenalin during the ordeal of being tied up.

She looked at the glowing end of the cigarette. It seemed to be approaching the cotton strip at an alarming rate of speed. *Okay, think!* she commanded her brain.

She could flip her wrist and toss the cigarette away from the pile of tissue paper, but it would still catch the carpet on fire. If she dropped the cigarette on the tissue paper, could she stand the heat long enough for it to burn the strip that held her wrist to the bed frame? She didn't really think so. But she *had* to do something!

Where was the nosy Mrs. Andrews when you needed her? And where were all these other folks who had watched over her like a hawk? Tony? Mom? Jim?

*Okay, be fair,* Lana admonished herself. She'd actually allowed herself to get into this mess. She should have known something was wrong when that cop wouldn't let her go back for her purse. But that wasn't solving her present problem.

Clasping her fingers tightly around the cigarette, she tested the strip of sheet holding her wrist. Tight. Dan had done a very good job tying it. There was no wiggle room. She glanced over the edge of the bed again. But there *was* one end of the strip hanging down toward the cigarette. Could she twist her hand far enough back to catch that end on fire? If so, she might be able to burn the tie off her wrist. Then maybe she could untie her feet and get free.

She tested the angle of the cigarette. No. The end of the cigarette wouldn't reach the end of the rope, and she couldn't twist her hand any further.

She leaned back on her pillow and screamed. But the stuffing in her mouth muffled her scream.

For a brief few seconds tears rolled out of Lana's eyes. No! She didn't have time for self-pity! She *had* to get out of this house!

Near panic, she tried to kick her feet. The tie around her ankles felt as if it slipped a little. She kicked again and felt the same movement. Was there hope? She began bucking her body up and down on the bed, like a horse trying to buck off its offending rider. Each time she tried to pull her knees up toward her body, the ankle ties seem to slip a little.

Lana became so involved with getting her feet free that she forgot the cigarette in her right hand. Suddenly heat engulfed her hand and she screamed. She'd dropped the cigarette and it had ignited the pile of tissue paper.

Frantically she pulled at her arm, trying to free it. Trying to move it. And suddenly it was free! The fire had burned the tie that was holding her to the bed. But pain encased her hand and wrist, almost debilitating her.

But she must get out of the house! The fire was lapping at the bed beside her, now. Sitting up, she pulled frantically at the tie around her ankles with her free hand. Tears ran down her face from the pain in her hand. And now she could feel heat from the fire beside her. Glancing around, she saw that the side of the bed was now beginning to flame.

Scooting herself toward the end of the bed, still mummy-wrapped except for her free arm and burned hand, she kept working at the tie that held her to the bed. If she could just get that tie loose, she could hop until she found a place to untie the one that actually held her ankles together. Finally she felt the tie come undone.

She turned to roll off the bed so she could run from the house, and only then realized that the entire side of the room toward the door was blazing. She immediately rolled toward the window. Sitting on the side of the bed, she managed to use her burned hand to open the window. She shoved at the screen, but it stayed in place.

The open window acted like a vent for the fire, and Lana suddenly felt the heat at her back. She lunged through the screen and landed in a thud on the ground. Thank goodness, the window wasn't far off the ground.

Knowing that she had to get away from the burning house, she managed to stand up and hop a few feet before she tripped and took a nosedive into the cedar tree near the house. Thankfully it was an evergreen, large enough to shelter her from flying cinders and sparks from the burning house. She hoped it wouldn't catch on fire.

She heard sirens in the distance and knew someone had called the fire department. Could any of her house be saved if they got here in time? Maybe half of it, but she was sure her bedroom was totally gone.

Three fire trucks roared onto her street. She tried to stand up and go meet the firemen, but found that she couldn't get up. She'd landed on her free arm, and it seemed to be pinned under her. She'd fallen headlong into the cedar and wound up under a low-hanging limb that now kept her from sitting up. With the other hand still tied up in the sheet, she couldn't move the limb enough to sit up. And she couldn't call out to them because the gag was still in her mouth. Besides that, even if she yelled her lungs out, they couldn't hear her over the sirens.

She became mesmerized, watching the firemen dash back and forth putting the fire out. Finally they had the fire under control and turned off the sirens.

"Was anyone in the house?" one of them asked.

"I don't know. The fire obviously started in the bedroom, since that's the main room that's been destroyed, but it's been totally charcoaled. If anyone was in the bed, they didn't make it."

Just then another car screeched to the curb and Tony jumped from it. "Where's Lana?" he yelled.

"Who's Lana?" one of the firemen called back to him. "So you know who lives here?"

"Lana Clarke lives here. Was she here? Has anyone seen her?" Panic made his voice gruff.

Lana tried to scream through the gag. The only sound was a guttural noise that didn't make it to the men. *I'm over here, Tony!* She tried to send him mental telepathy. But he headed inside the house instead of coming to her.

"You can't go in there!" a fireman yelled at him, grabbing his arm. Tony yanked his arm away from the fireman and proceeded into the house.

All the while she watched, Lana kept trying to sit up. Her burned hand was hurting so badly she felt faint. If she could back out of the shrub the way she fell into it, maybe she could get their attention.

She was beginning to crawfish out a little at a time when something in the shadows of the house next door caught her eye. Another car pulling up to the curb lit the shadows enough for her to recognize Dan Smith before he ducked back into the deeper shadows.

He was actually watching and enjoying the situation. What a sick human being! But suddenly Lana realized she needed to stay out of sight for now. She didn't want Dan to know she'd made it out of the fire. Had he seen her jump from the window? Was that why he was hanging around? If so, then he might know she was in the cedar.

Detective Collins got out of the car that had just pulled up. He said a few words to the firemen, then went inside the house to find Tony. Soon he reappeared leading Tony by the arm.

"Look, man," he was saying, "we don't know if she was in there or not. I know you found her cell phone and purse at her mom's, but she may have gone anywhere."

"No. Not Lana. She'd never leave the house without her purse. She was forcefully brought here. I know it!" And he sank to his knees and covered his face. Lana could see his shoulders shaking.

She had to get to him! She had to let him know she was okay, whether Dan saw her or not. Frantically she started trying to back out of the cedar again. Suddenly she felt two large hands grab her feet and pull her from the tree. She looked up into the eyes of Tom Hoover.

"Don't say anything," he whispered. He lifted her and tossed her over his shoulder, then quickly made his way to the back of her house, where he cut through a neighbor's yard to the adjoining street. He dumped her into the back of what appeared to be a utility van, got in and drove away.

After a few miles Tom stopped in a dark area and opened the back of the van and got in, closing the door behind him. "This is going to hurt me more than it is you," he said, snatching the tape from her mouth. The material that Tom was in the process of pulling out of her mouth muffled her yelp.

"Hang on," he said to Lana, then answered his cell phone. "Yes, she's here. I'm in the process of untying her. Okay." He handed the phone to Lana. She could barely hold the phone with her burned, aching hand.

"Baby, are you okay?" Tony's voice was gruff with worry.

"Yes, but how did you know Tom had me? I saw you at my house. I was trying to let you know I was okay when Tom rescued me."

"I know. Tom is taking you to the hospital now. I'm on my way. We'll explain everything then."

"Does Mom know I'm alright?"

"Yes, she's on her way to the hospital to meet us. I have to go. I'll see you in a little while."

All the time she'd talked on the phone, Tom had been unwinding the mummy sheet from her. "You stay back here, just in case someone sees me. I don't want you to be seen until we get to the hospital."

"Tom?" She stopped him as he turned to leave the van.

"Yes?"

"Up until recently, I'd never pictured my guardian angel to be a big black man. Thank you for continuing to rescue me." Tears of gratitude slid down her face.

"It's my understanding that guardian angels come in all sizes, shapes and colors," Tom said, gently wiping the tears from her face. "And the rescuing part is all my pleasure. But now I have to finish my mission and get you to the hospital. If Tony gets there before I do, I'm afraid my wings might get clipped."

**In a few minutes** Tom pulled into the emergency area of the Springhill Medical Center. Before he could get out of the van the back door was snatched open and two men wearing lab coats were reaching for Lana.

They helped her from the van, sat her in a wheelchair and rolled her into the emergency room, then quickly into a sectioned-off area. She was helped to a sitting position on the bed.

"The doctor will be with you shortly," one of the men said.

A doctor and nurse showed up almost immediately. "Oh my goodness! Look at this hand," the nurse gasped to the doctor.

For the first time Lana looked at her hand, and immediately fainted.

# *Chapter 16*

**"Lana, wake up.** Come on, honey, wake up, you're okay."

Lana drifted slowly from the dark and became aware of the stranger in white hovering over her, patting her cheeks.

Then everything came rushing back to her. Her eyes popped open and landed on her mom and Tony, standing a little distance from the doctor and nurse who were examining her.

"Here she is," the nurse announced.

"Good girl!" the doctor said in his medically patronizing way. "Okay, Mom and Tony, I'm going to let you two have a few words with her, then I need to run a few tests on this hand and see what we need to do." He left the room.

Alma hugged Lana as tears flowed down her face. "Oh, baby, I was so horrified that we'd lost you—" She broke down and couldn't go on.

"Mom, I'm okay. I'll tell you all about it when the doctor finishes with me. Look, let's let the doctor finish with me so I can go home. That sounds really good to me right now." Although sadness filled her when she remembered it would be a while before she could go to her own house.

"She's right, Alma," Tony said. "Jenny and Hank are in the waiting room. Let them take you home. I'll wait and bring Lana home when the doctor finishes. As you can see, she's going to be fine."

He leaned over and kissed Lana gently on the lips. She saw tears pool in his eyes as he tried to say something. Words wouldn't form around the lump in his throat, so he wrapped his arms around her and held her tightly against him.

"Okay, folks," the doctor said, breezing back into the room. "Let me check this hand out a little more, then I think Lana can go home."

**At home in her bed,** Lana was wide awake. Her mom, Jim, Jenny and Hank had been waiting when she got home. She'd relayed the entire story to them. Even when repeating the story, the horror of what had almost happened to her hadn't sunk in. But now, alone in her room, it had.

Two times, now, she'd almost died at the hands of Dan Smith. Would he finally succeed? Supposedly he didn't know she was still alive. He thought she'd died in the fire, unless he saw her jump from the window. But he'd thought she'd died at sea, too. So how long would it take for the news to get back to him that she was still alive? And how long would it be before he tried to kill her again?

Her hand hurt. The doctor said she had second-degree burns, but didn't think there would be any scarring. He gave her some samples of salve to put on her hand until she could get her prescription filled. But it wasn't the pain from the burns that kept her awake.

After turning and tossing for what seemed like forever, she finally got up. She'd go to the kitchen and get some milk. Maybe that would help settle her nerves.

But what she really wanted was to be close to Tony. Somehow, that's the only way she would feel safe tonight.

She bypassed the kitchen and walked down the hall to the guestroom. The door was closed, so she quietly eased it open and just as quietly closed it behind her. She could hear his rhythmic breathing. Being careful not to wake him, she eased into the bed beside him. It would be enough just to lie beside him and feel his warm presence.

Lying on her side, facing away from him, she settled into place.

She closed her eyes and took a deep breath. Now she could sleep.

His arm came around her waist as he said, "I've fantasized about this every night since I've been here."

"I thought you were asleep!" she said, feeling embarrassed now that she'd been caught.

"Nope. Can't sleep. I'm lying here figuring ways to destroy Dan Smith."

"I couldn't sleep, either. I kept reliving being tied up and thinking I would burn to death."

"Well, you didn't burn to death. And now I know how Mary died. I knew she didn't go to sleep smoking a cigarette. But I don't want to talk about all that, now that I have you in my bed." He pulled her closer to him and nuzzled his nose in the back of her neck. "I have a terrible dilemma. I desperately want to make love to you, but I know how your mom feels about it. Do you have any suggestions?"

Lana turned her face toward him and welcomed his kiss. As his lips softly played with hers, his hand worked its way to her breasts and was driving her mad with desire. When he broke the kiss long enough to nibble down her neck, she managed to whisper, "Tony?"

"Hmm?"

"Tony! Can we just hold each other tonight? When we make love for the first time, I want my mind totally on you and nothing else. But tonight I keep having flashes of Dan hovering over me, rolling me up in that damn sheet."

"I understand. I wasn't going to dishonor your mom's wishes, anyway. I just had to have a taste of you. Try to sleep, now. I'm here and I can promise you that Dan Smith can't touch you tonight." He gave her one more lingering kiss, "To remember me by," he said, then rested his head beside hers, on her pillow.

**A loud pounding on the door** brought Tony and Lana quickly awake. "Tony! Tony!" Alma was yelling, "Lana's not in her room! Tony, she's been taken!" And she burst through the door.

"Oooh!" she mouthed, looking into the startled eyes of the two in the bed. "I'm so sorry! I went to your room to take you a cup of coffee and you weren't there, so I panicked."

"Mom, it's not what it looks like. I couldn't sleep, so I came in here. But nothing happened." Lana felt like a teenager caught making out in her bedroom.

"Then maybe I need to leave so you can remedy that situation," Alma said. "Coffee is ready when you two decide you want some. Detective Collins called and said he'd be over here at ten to talk with you about last night." With a huge smile, she closed the door behind her.

"Well, I do believe we just got permission to be promiscuous," Tony said, pulling Lana close.

But Lana scooted to the edge of the bed and stood up. "I've got to get out of here before she thinks we did!" she said, walking to the door. "I couldn't face my mom if she thought I'd been naughty in her house."

"So after we're married, if we ever spend the night here I can't make love to you?"

Tony looked breathtakingly sexy sitting on the side of the bed in nothing except his boxers, with his hair tousled from the night's sleep.

In a daring move, Lana went back to the bed and took a clump of his tangled hair in her left hand, tilting his head back so she could look in his eyes. She was standing between his legs. "Mr. Angelino, after we're married, you can make love to me anywhere you feel brave enough to do it! So was that a proposal?"

Still holding a handful of hair, she kissed him long and hard while rubbing her breasts tantalizingly on his chest. Feeling his hands slowly wrap around her waist, she stepped quickly back from him and headed for the door.

"Tease!" he called after her. "So was that a yes?"

"Maybe. Depends on the size of the ring that goes with it," she said, as she smiled and left the room.

**Again the group sat around** Alma's dining room table. And again Lana repeated her story of the day before.

Detective Collins had agreed to wait until this morning to take the report. After Lana told him everything she could remember and answered all his questions, she asked, "So what about the burglary call you all went out on? Did you catch Maxie breaking into a house?"

Detective Collins looked at Tony, then back at Lana. "It was all a farce. The entire thing was a way to get our attention away from you so Dan could get his hands on you."

"You mean the emails and website that Ron found were fake, too?"

"Yes. Maxie is working with Dan, and she used Ron to get to you. But the good news is, Ron is innocent. That first email he got was deliberately sent to him."

"So where does that leave us?"

"We tried picking Maxie up at work this morning, but she wasn't there. We're checking out her apartment now."

"Does Ron know he was used?"

"Yes. But we asked him to go on to work and act naturally, in case Maxie showed up."

"So what do we do now?" Lana asked.

"We find Dan and his goons and bring them in," Detective Collins said.

"Are we still being watched from next door?" she asked.

"That problem is solved, I believe," Detective Collins answered. "It seems that Julian Johnson, the great-grandson of the woman who owned the house, and who inherited it when she died, was renting the house to Maxie. He claims he didn't know what was going on at the house. But assured me he would stop renting it to Maxie."

"Julian Johnson is one of my managers," Tony said. "Lana and I saw him talking with Maxie one day, but I didn't think much more about it. Do you think he's innocent, or should I fire him?"

"We sent a couple of officers to question him, and he seems innocent. If we turn up anything I'll let you know. In the meantime, I'd leave him alone. If you have another employee that you really trust, you might ask them to keep an eye on him to see if Maxie shows back up."

"How can we be sure he'll stop renting it?" Alma asked. "What if Maxie puts pressure on him and he caves in? I won't rest easy until I know I can be out in my front yard and not feel eyes on me."

Lana noticed Jim's hand reach out and gently squeeze Alma's arm.

"Can we board the house up?" Jim asked. "If Julian doesn't know what's going on at his rental house, he won't know we've eliminated the chance of any rats getting in."

"Well, we shouldn't tamper with someone else's property without them knowing it, but we'll watch it closely, Mrs. Clarke, and if you see any suspicious activity, just let me know."

"I'll do better than that," Tony spoke up. "I'll go today and get a surveillance camera and mount it on this house. That way we can keep up with any goings-on over there."

"That's a good idea, Tony. But don't buy one. Come by the station and I'll loan you one. You can hook it up through your home computer."

After the meeting was over and Detective Collins had left, Lana said, "Tony, I want to go to my house. I need to see what kind of damage was done."

"Lana, honey, don't do that. It's just going to upset you," Alma pleaded.

"I know it will upset me, but I'm already upset. I'm upset at this whole thing. So seeing my house won't make it any worse."

"But you can't do that," Tony interrupted. "You have to stay hidden so Dan will think he's really killed you."

"Well, hell! Why don't we just plan my funeral? That will make it really believable!" Frustration vibrated in her voice.

"You know, that's not a bad idea!" Tony said.

"What?" Lana and Alma chorused.

"Wait, ladies. Let Tony talk," Jim said. "What do you have in mind?"

"I don't know. Lana just gave me the idea, but I think we should brainstorm this. At least hang a wreath on the door. And I know the editor of the *Press-Register*. I might be able to talk him into running a fake obit."

Lana listened to the two men with her mouth open. They were going to kill her off! Her friends would read the obituary and think she was dead.

"Look, I'm going down to the station and get that camera. I'll talk with Detective Collins about this and see what he thinks. In the meantime, Lana, it's imperative that you don't leave the house. Absolutely nobody can see you."

"Look, I don't want to do this!" She finally found her voice. "There has to be a better way."

"You want Dan caught, don't you?" Tony asked, placing his arm around her shoulders. "If he can feel sure that you're really dead, he'll start getting sloppy. We'll have a much better chance of catching him."

"Tony, I just can't stand the idea of not being able to leave the house. It gives me claustrophobia just thinking about it."

"I understand that. But let me work on this plan first, then I'll figure out a way to get you out of the house. How's that?"

"Okay," Lana agreed. "I guess I can die for a little while."

"That's my girl," Tony said, and placed a soft kiss on her lips.

**A couple of hours later** Lana was in the living room reading a book while Alma and Jim sat at the dining room table designing flower boxes for the front windows. She heard a car door slam and assumed Tony was home. But a gentle knock on the door told her differently.

She stepped to the kitchen and said, "Mom, someone's at the door. Since I'm dead, I don't need to answer it."

"Lana! I hate hearing you say that," Alma protested, and went to the door. Jim was close on her heels. Lana stayed out of sight.

Soon Jim and Alma came back into the dining room. Tears flowed down Alma's face as she pulled Lana to her and held her tightly. "This makes it too real," she wept.

Looking over Alma's shoulder, Lana raised questioning eyebrows at Jim.

"They just hung a wreath on the door," he said.

# Chapter 17

"**Okay, here's the plan,**" Tony said, placing a bag from Angelino's on the table and reaching into it. "Here we have a long blond wig. I think this will look wonderful on you." He grinned at Lana. "You'll be a Dolly Parton look-alike."

Jenny, Hank, Alma and Jim all laughed. But Lana just looked at Tony. What was he doing now?

"Anyway, the plan is this. You wear this wig and these sunshades," he said, pulling out the largest pair of gaudy sunshades Lana had ever seen. "We're going to sneak you out through the back patio and into the van I rented. Hank is going to drive you over to my house, where you'll stay until this is all over. Since you've never been to my house, there'll be a lot to explore, so hopefully you won't get bored."

"So this is all happening—when? Now? With only a two-minute notice? When am I supposed to pack? What am I supposed to pack? And for how long?"

"Yes. Now. As little as possible, and indefinitely." Tony answered all her questions at once, to the delight of the others.

But before Lana could get upset, he added, "Hank and I are going to mount this surveillance camera into the wreath, then hook it up to the computer, so that will take awhile. You have plenty of time to throw some things together. You won't need much, since you won't have to dress up. Just a few nighties," he finished, giving her a big wink.

Dodging the punch that Lana slung his way, Tony immediately became involved with rigging the camera.

"Lana, let Jenny and me help you pack some things," Alma said, touching Lana's cheek. It was becoming harder and harder for her to watch her daughter be in danger. She was happy Tony was taking Lana to his house. She felt Lana would be much safer there.

In her room, Lana stood in front of her closet staring at the clothes. What was she supposed to take to Tony's? How long would she be there? She plopped down on the side of her bed in pure frustration.

"Here you go," Alma said, coming into the room with a suitcase. "This won't be as conspicuous as hanging clothes. Would you like for me to pack you some things?"

"I don't know where to start, Mom," Lana said. "I just don't know where to start." She flinched as a pain shot through her burnt hand.

"Okay, that's it," Alma said. "Jenny, you pack her toiletries. Just take everything from the bathroom. That way she'll have anything she needs. I'll pick out some clothes and put them in the suitcase."

Lana watched in a surreal mood as Alma and Jenny prepared for her to move in with Tony. Little jittery flutters passed through her at the thought of being alone with Tony at his house.

How long would she have to stay "dead" and hide out at this house? How long would it be before she could see her mom and Jenny again?

"I can't come to see you, Mom. And you can't come to see me! Jenny, you may have the baby before I'm allowed to come back from the dead! I hate this. I'm not going to do this!" she said, getting up from the bed. "I'm telling Tony that I don't want to roll over and play dead."

"But Lana, you'll be safer this way," Alma reasoned. "I'm so tired of worrying about you. Please do this for a few days, just to give them a chance to find Dan. Please. Do it so I can relax a little about you."

Lana saw the worry lines around her mom's eyes and mouth and knew she'd give in.

"Okay, Mom. But just for a few days. A week at the most. Then if Detective Collins and his mighty warriors haven't found Dan Smith, I'm going after him myself."

"And she will, too," Alma said to Tony, who had just come into the room in time to hear Lana's declaration.

**Hank, wearing coveralls and a cap** that declared "Plumbing's my life,'" drove a van with the same slogan on both sides of it while Lana sat in the back on some boxes. She only had the faintest idea where she was being taken, because she could only see the top of the tallest buildings as they passed through Mobile.

Finally the van stopped and Hank rolled his window down. "I'm here to work on Anthony Angelino's plumbing," he said to the attendant in the guardhouse.

"Okay, go ahead. Mr. Angelino said you were coming."

After driving past the guardhouse, Hank said, "Okay, you can sit up and look around, Lana. You need to see Tony's house and some of the property as we approach it. This is an estate that's been in his family since his grandparents came here from Italy. Tuscany, to be exact. Tony's grandfather left this place to him, but Tony hasn't lived here much in the past few years, even though he loves it. Tony's mom died when he was a teenager, and his dad died two years later. Tony's grandfather raised him, right here."

They were on a well-paved road that twined through and under huge oak trees that formed a tunnel over the road. Blue-gray Spanish moss hung from the trees like tentacles reaching down to welcome them. After driving about a fourth of a mile through the trees, the van came into an opening that looked as if they had gone through a time warp and landed in another world. Another country.

On each side of the road, slightly sloping terrain was covered with grape vineyards. Lana had heard of the muscadine grapes that did so well in the area, but she'd never seen any actually growing.

Since it was spring, the vines were covered in new leaves and blooms.

"Tony makes most of his own wine from these muscadine grapes," Hank said. "That's some good wine, too. We've encouraged him to sell it, but he enjoys just having it for friends and family.

"And that's his house," Hank said, pointing to a large two-story Italian-style farmhouse. "His grandfather came from farmers in the old country, and even though he'd made it rich in America, he wanted to reflect his roots."

Lana watched in amazement as they approached the house, which was built from light-colored, rough-hewed stone. The sun glinted off the stone, causing Lana to ask, "Is the house built from granite?"

"Yes. Tony's grandfather had the stones brought from North Carolina. He wanted the house to look like the granite houses in Italy, but knew it would be less expensive to have the stones put on railcars and brought from North Carolina, rather than shipping them from Italy."

A front porch ran the length of the lower level, and a balcony ran the length of the upper level. Thick wooden posts supported the porch and balcony, and wood-stained rockers were grouped around small marble tables, creating seating areas along the length of the porch. A swing hung from each end of the porch. A person could spend hours on that porch, reading, visiting, or just day-dreaming, Lana thought.

As Hank stopped the van in front of the house, Tony came out of one of the three doors that opened onto the porch. He helped Lana out of the van.

"Welcome home," he said simply, as he took her in his arms and kissed her. "I wanted to be the one to give you your first glimpse of the house, but this way was the best, under the circumstances."

"Can you come in?" he asked Hank after he ended the bone-melting kiss he'd given Lana.

"No, I need to get this van back and take Jenny home. She's been tired a lot lately. She needs her rest."

"You're beginning to sound like an old married man," Tony joked, and took Hank into a bear hug. "Thanks for helping me rescue my fair damsel," he added, releasing Hank.

"My pleasure, my friend. Lana, don't let him take advantage of you, all alone in this big house. There are plenty of rooms where you can hide if he starts annoying you."

"I'll keep that in mind," Lana laughed.

They watched Hank drive away, then Tony draped his arm around Lana's shoulder and led her up the steps. Before they reached the door Lana removed the blond wig and let the balmy breeze fluff her own hair. The scent of fresh blooms and the countryside filled her with pure joy.

"This is a beautiful place, Tony," she said in awe.

"Thanks. I hope you like it. It was my grandfather's pride and joy. He loved it because it's built on the same scale and decorated just like the one he grew up in. I've always loved it here. Little did I dream that it would one day be mine. I hope you like the inside, too. We can always redecorate, but I've never really wanted to change it."

He opened the door and they entered another world.

Lana stood in awe as she looked around the huge room. Eggshell-colored stucco walls cast a warm glow everywhere. Heavy beams across the ceiling gave the room a feeling of sturdiness and home. The room was tastefully decorated with Italian designs. Hand-painted pictures hung from the walls and ceramics from, Lana was sure, different parts of Italy, were placed on shelves.

Two huge sofas angled to a stone fireplace that would add warmth and comfort in the winter months. The floors were stone, but colorful throw rugs in key spots added texture and ambience to the room.

Tony led Lana to the next room, which was the kitchen. She realized the entire kitchen wall facing outside was glass, looking out over another porch. And as she let her gaze go farther, she knew she was looking at the waters of the Gulf of Mexico.

The kitchen had all modern appliances, yet maintained the same old country look as the living room. This held true as Tony showed her the entire house. It was totally modern, yet appeared to be straight out of Tuscany.

There were four bedrooms, each with its own bath. Tony explained where all the furniture had come from. He showed her his grandparents' favorite rooms and their bedroom, which was now his.

"We'll tour the outside later, but look out this window," he said, drawing her to a ceiling-to-floor window in his bedroom and pulling the drapes back.

Lana looked down at a large mandolin-shaped swimming pool with a hot tub adjoining it. Surrounding the pool was a beautiful flower garden filled with azaleas, roses, pansies, and other blooms she didn't recognize.

"Don't tell me you take care of the garden?" she asked.

"No, Gonzalo is my gardener. He got his training working in the Bellingrath Gardens, so he's very good. He also takes care of the pool and hot tub. You'll usually see him somewhere in the garden and yard any day of the week. Sunday is his day off, but he can't seem to stay away from 'his babies,' as he calls the garden and flowers. His mother was from Mexico and his dad was French. He's quite a character."

Even as Tony talked, a figure wearing a sombrero and huge dark sunshades came around a corner and started examining the flowers. He had a handlebar mustache and wore loose-fitting white pants and shirt.

"There he is now," Tony said. "He keeps that mustache trimmed as meticulously as he does my boxwoods."

"How much property do you own?" Lana asked.

"Two hundred acres."

"How do you know someone isn't coming on your property? I know you have the guardhouse, but couldn't someone come over a fence somewhere else?"

"Not my fences." Tony's voice held the slightest hint of sarcasm. "When Mary and I got married, she said the only way she'd live out here was to have electric fences put around the entire property to keep prowlers out. So I had 10-foot electric fences installed along with the guardhouse, with 24/7 guards. After I'd spent a small fortune doing that, she still refused to live here. That's when I gave in and bought the house closer to town. Until Dan Smith tried to kill you in the Bahamas, I didn't use guards anymore. But knowing that eventually I wanted you to be here, I started using them again."

When they'd made their way back downstairs to the living room, Tony put his hands on Lana's shoulders and turned her to him. "Don't you like it? You haven't said very much."

"Tony, I'm in shock. I don't know where to start. You're so modern acting and you *own* Angelino's department store. And yet your house is so warm and inviting and—and other than the quiet, understated elegance, it's almost simple. It really *is* like a farmhouse. I just wouldn't have ever guessed that you lived in a house like this. When you said your house had a guard, I assumed you lived in a gated community. You know, one of those huge, cold, expensive houses with no character.

"I mean—" she turned around in several circles, taking everything in, "this would be such a wonderful place to raise kids!" Realizing what she'd said, Lana felt her face burn hot. She'd forgotten about Gino.

"My dream has always been to have this house full of kids," Tony said. "My kids and their friends. I can see them running everywhere. But Mary hated this house. We never lived here. She picked out the house we lived in, and the one she ultimately died in. She said she'd never live in this old piece of junk."

"Oh, Tony. I'm so sorry. This is a magnificent house. It would be such a joy to live in a house like this."

"Remember the other morning at your mom's, you said your answer was 'yes' to my proposal, depending on the size of the stone?" Tony asked.

"You know I was kidding about a stone," Lana said.

"Is this one big enough?" Tony asked, taking her hand and sliding a ring on her finger.

Lana stared open-mouthed at the most beautiful ring she'd ever seen. Sapphire and emerald swirls encircled a diamond that rested in the center. The diamond itself had to be at least two carats.

"It was my grandmother's," Tony said. "It would honor me, and her, if you would wear it. Lana, will you marry me? Will you have my babies and raise them here with me? Will you be by my side until death takes one of us? Will you make me the happiest man on earth?

"I love you, Lana. I think I've loved you ever since I walked into your mom's house that first night and saw that determined, defiant, yet slightly hurt look in your eyes. I've wanted to be a part of your world, ever since."

Tears ran gently down Lana's face as she turned it up to him. "Oh, yes, Tony. I'll marry you. I'll have our babies and raise them here. And I'll be by your side until death takes one of us. And if I go first, I'll wait for you to join me. And Tony, I'll do all of that without a ring. But if you want me to, I'll wear this ring in memory of the woman's blood that runs through your veins. And I'll wear it in honor of you.

"I think I've loved you ever since you blatantly fed me pie, just to spite poor Jenny." She paused, then asked hesitantly, "Tony, will you make love with me?"

"I thought you'd never ask," he whispered against her upturned lips.

Knowing they were finally alone, with nobody to accidentally walk in on them, Lana relaxed and allowed her emotions and thoughts to revolve solely around Tony.

She couldn't foretell the future, but she knew she loved this man, and apparently he loved her, in spite of the fact that she was not slim and trim like the fashion models splashed everywhere one looked. Lana was still in awe that once she'd stopped worrying about her weight and trying to have a body she was never meant to have, Tony came along to fullfill all her fantasies.

She entwined her hands in Tony's hair, drawing him closer trying to deepen the kiss. But he insisted on dropping feather kisses on her face, her eyelids, her neck, and finally the corners of her mouth. He was driving her crazy with desire. She strained her body ever closer to his, hoping to mold and become one with him.

But his lips continued to nibble and toy with her. He gently brushed his mouth back and forth across hers, and when she parted her lips, trying to receive his kiss, he caught her bottom lip and gently sucked it. Finally he claimed her lips with his.

Lana felt her entire body opening for this man. Her heart, her soul, her body was ready to receive all the love he had to give, and to give all she had to give, in return.

His hands roamed her body. Each touch was a caress. She hadn't known that a simple touch could convey such love. That a simple stroke could articulate unspoken words.

Slowly, Tony held her slightly from him. "As much as I want you right now, I want our first time to be in that bedroom upstairs that was my grandparents'. I want our marriage to be as happy as theirs was. So I want to wait until our wedding night to make love with you in that room. But I promise you it will be worth the wait. I'm going to love you all night long.

"I love your body, Lana. I love the soft feel of your curves. I love the way you respond to me. I love the way our bodies fit together when I'm holding you. But more than your body, I love who you are." He placed one hand on her temple and the other on her heart. "I love the person that I know lives in here. Your body is only the vehicle that transports the person that I love.

"I love your zest for life. Your stubbornness. Your soft, loving side. So if you gain another hundred pounds or lose a hundred pounds, that won't affect my love for you. Do you believe that?"

"Oh, Tony. Are you really real? You must be a figment of my imagination. I've only dreamed that a man like you existed. But now I've found you. Yes, I do believe you. You have no reason to lie to me. But, know this—if you ever try to get away from me, I'll break both your legs. I'll make Kathy Bates in the movie *Misery* look tame." But the kiss she gave him said she'd never do anything to hurt him.

"Even your torture would be sweet to me," he whispered gruffly. "But we'd better go see what's in the kitchen cabinets for dinner, or I may break my word about waiting until our wedding night to love you."

# Chapter 18

"**Is Detective Collins getting any closer to finding Dan?**" Lana asked Tony. A week had passed since she'd come to stay with him. A week of mixed emotions for Lana. She had fallen in love with his house and gardens, but she resented the fact that she was a prisoner in this paradise. She hadn't seen her mom or Jenny in a week, and she missed them.

"No. It's as if Dan has disappeared from the face of the earth. Tom has even lost him. I didn't want to tell you because it's so frustrating," Tony answered.

They had just finished breakfast and Tony was going to the office. "I'm sorry, baby. I know this is unbearable for you, but we can't do anything about it right now. We have to make everything look natural. If your mom or Jenny comes here and any of his people are watching, then they'll be suspicious.

"I know this is really hard on your mom with all the calls she's getting concerning your obituary in the paper. I'm so sorry she can't call you. But if they've tapped her phone lines then they would know you're alive, so we can't take that chance."

"I know. I just get so exasperated knowing that Dan Smith is still free to come and go as he wishes, but I'm in hiding. Don't get me wrong, Tony. This is the most wonderful place I could ever dream of hiding in, but it's just the principle, I guess."

"It will soon be over," Tony promised, gathering her close and kissing her. "I won't be at the office but a couple of hours. When I get back, if you want to, we'll get Gonzalo to drive us around the property on his golf cart."

"That sounds wonderful," Lana beamed. Suddenly the day seemed brighter.

## After Tony left, Lana sat at the kitchen bar and sipped on another

cup of coffee. This week with Tony had been wonderful. He was loving and attentive. In the evenings they would snuggle on the couch and watch TV or just talk. Most nights ended with the snuggling getting too hot and heavy and Tony would lead them upstairs to separate bedrooms. Lana wondered if he was as frustrated as she was.

She glanced around the kitchen. It was an eat-in kitchen. A small dining room table with six chairs was in the middle of the room. It was meant for cozy family gatherings when the large formal dining room that adjoined the kitchen wasn't needed. Cabinets and counter space surrounded the room. The gas stove was designed to look like an old woodburning stove. The refrigerator was designed to look like an antique pie safe. One had to open the screen door to get to the door of the refrigerator. The décor reminded Lana of going to her great-grandmother's home when she was a small child.

The knock on the back door brought Lana out of her reverie. Startled, she eased to the door and peeked out. Gonzalo stood just outside the door. The large sombrero shaded his face, but he looked apologetic for disturbing her.

Opening the door, she said, "Hi, Gonzalo, I'm Lana. What do you need?"

Gonzalo stepped quickly inside the door and closed it. Then he tossed the sombrero to the floor. "I need for you to die, bitch!" Dan Smith's voice came from behind the handlebar mustache.

"Dan! What have you done with Gonzalo?" Lana demanded. Fear for herself was second place to her concern for the gardener.

"You don't worry about that mixed-breed," Dan said. "You're the hardest damn woman to kill that I've ever seen. But as the old saying goes, three times a charm." His voice was hard and bitter.

"How did you get past the guard?" Lana asked.

"You shut up, right now! You and that mouth of yours won't get one word out of me. I've already been there with you."

While he talked, Lana visually searched him for a weapon. She couldn't find anything, but the loose-fitting white clothing could easily be hiding a gun. She frantically tried to think of a weapon she could fight back with.

Her cell phone was in the left pocket of her slacks. Could she open it and dial Tony's number on the speed dial? She had him programmed on #3, so she might be able to do it.

She eased the phone from her pocket and slid back onto the stool where she'd been drinking coffee earlier. Trying to look nonchalant, she drooped her left hand down beside her and lifted the coffee cup with her right hand.

"You look real relaxed to be about to die," Dan sneered.

She casually lifted her cup to her lips and took a sip. "I'm just trying to figure out how you plan to kill me," she answered, while she slid her thumb along the first row of numbers on the phone. When she found #3—she prayed it was #3—she pushed it, then found the "send" button with her thumb and pushed that. *God, please don't let this go into his voicemail,* she prayed.

Slowly Dan slid a derringer from a front pocket of the pants, and a ball of boxing twine from the other pocket. "These baggy clothes come in real handy," he smirked.

"So let me get this straight," Lana said in a voice she raised in hopes that Tony could hear her, if he had answered his phone. "You're going to tie me up, then shoot me, Dan? Or are you going to shoot me, then tie me up?"

"I told you to shut your mouth!" he yelled, stepping closer to her. "Just stand up and follow me."

Lana slid off the bar stool with her left side away from him. She slid the open phone back into her pocket.

"Now put your hands behind you," he ordered, shaking the twine loose with one hand, still holding the derringer on her with his other.

Suddenly the pent up fury that had been with Lana since her episode with Dan in the Bahamas rose to the surface. The days she'd had to hide out from him and his goons. The danger he had put her mom and sister in. She knew he'd have to be close to kill her with a derringer. But at this point she was willing to take her chances. She'd had enough of Dan Smith, and she didn't plan to watch as he tied her up a second time.

"Turn around and put your hands behind you, I said. If I have to tell you a second time, I'll shoot you in the head."

"So what? If I'm going to die, do you really think I care how I die? You'll either shoot me or whatever it is you're going to do when you get me tied up, so what do I care?"

"TURN AROUND!" Dan screamed. His face was beet red with anger.

Lana smiled into his enraged eyes, slowly turning her back to him. But in mid-turn she came up with her right arm, knocking the derringer from his hand. Before he could gain control she shoved him backwards against the table. She grabbed the bar stool she'd just been sitting on and brought it down across his shoulders, forcing him to the floor.

Scrambling, he tried to get away from her so he could stand up. He frantically searched the room for his gun.

But Lana didn't care where the gun was. Once the rage started to pour from her, she couldn't stop. Before he could get further than his knees she brought the bar stool down against his head and shoulders. He fell to the floor, face down—motionless.

Had she killed him? The thought sobered Lana enough to bring some rationality to her. She grabbed the twine and, straddling Dan, sat down on him. If he tried to get up, at least her weight would pin him down momentarily.

Quickly she tied his wrists behind him. She tied his ankles together, then tied them to a leg of the table. It wouldn't hold him long, but maybe she'd have time to run to the guardhouse and get help.

She had just found the derringer when she heard pounding on the front door. Peeking though the window, she was relieved to see the guard standing outside. But *was* it the guard? By now she was afraid to open the door.

"Can I help you?" she called through the door.

"Ma'am, Tony called and said he thought you were in trouble. He's on his way with the police, but do you need my help?"

Tucking the derringer in her right pocket, she opened the door. "Yes, you can make sure the snake in the kitchen stays where he is until the police get here," she said, leading the way to the kitchen.

Dan still lay face down in the floor. "I may have killed him," Lana said, poking at him with her foot.

The guard leaned down and felt the pulse on Dan's neck. "Nope. It's beating just fine. I think he'll live to see jail time."

They heard sirens approaching. Tony rushed through the house first. When he saw Lana, he grabbed her to him. "Thank God you're okay. I was going crazy! I could hear you and some of what was going on, but you would never come back on the phone and say you were okay."

"I'm sorry. I got kind of busy and forgot about the phone," she said, pointing to Dan.

At that moment Detective Collins came to a sudden stop as he ran into the room. He and Tony spotted Dan at the same time, and erupted into gales of laughter.

"Tied up like a wild boar," the guard said. That's the way he was when I got here."

Dan started to moan and struggle to sit up. Tony reached down and took him by the hair and pulled him to a sitting position.

"What tha—???" Dan said when he saw everyone standing around him.

Tony crouched down to look him in the eyes. "Dan, I want nothing more than to kill you, right now, with my bare hands, but that would be too easy for you. I want you to spend the rest of your life in jail. And every time Big Bubba uses you, I want you to see my face."

"You have the right to remain silent—" Detective Collins began.

## "Is it really finally over?" Alma asked.

They were all gathered around her dining room table. Alma, Jim, Jenny, Hank, Tony and Lana. Just like that first night she'd met Tony, Lana thought. The only difference now was Jim. Even after the threat of Dan Smith had been eliminated, Jim kept coming over to see Alma.

"Yes. It's over," Tony said. "Dan has been charged with first-degree murder on one count and attempted murder on two counts. If Gonzalo hadn't been able to dial the police, he'd have died from the stab wound that Dan gave him when he broke into his home and stole his clothes."

"Oops! There she goes again," Hank said, putting his hand on Jenny's stomach. The baby, a girl, was making herself well known these days. Her movements were very visible through the knit top Jenny wore. "I'm sorry to interrupt, but I can't resist when I see her moving," Hank apologized.

"You're going to be such a good daddy," Alma said, then turned back to Tony. "What about Maxie?"

"Maxie and Ally's charges are pending. But I'm sure they'll both spend some time in jail for their parts in Dan's scheme."

A loud pounding on the front door startled them. Alma went to see who it was. They all heard Ron's voice and words. "Is Lana here? I've got to see her. She's had her cell phone number changed and I can't reach her."

Lana kissed Tony on the cheek as she got up from the table. "I'd better handle this," she said.

Alma left them alone in the living room. Ron caught Lana in a close hug. "I was so worried about you. I was going out of my mind! I hated seeing that obituary in the paper. It could have come true. I was afraid they were tempting fate to even have that thing printed."

Lana stepped out of his embrace. "I'm sorry you had to worry, Ron. But it's all over now. We can all relax. I've been meaning to thank you for the part you played by keeping quiet about the computers in the office."

"That was the least I could do. Baby, I've done a lot of thinking during all this. I love you. Will you marry me? I was a jerk about the weight. That doesn't matter to me. I just want you to be my wife."

"I'm so sorry, Ron. But I've already been taken," Lana said, holding up her hand with the beautiful antique ring Tony had given her.

Ron sat quickly down on the sofa, as if the wind had gone out of him. "I waited too long, didn't I? I was so stupid!" He buried his face in his hands.

Lana sat beside him and took one of his hands. "Think about it, Ron. During the year you and I dated, you never once tried to make love to me. You seldom ever even kissed me. Does that sound like love to you? I don't think you're in love with me. I think I'm just a comfortable habit for you. Go find someone you can feel passionate about. Find someone you really love."

"Did you ever love me, Lana?"

"I loved you—and still love you—in a familial way. Like I would a brother. But not like I want to love my husband. I'm sorry, Ron. It just wasn't meant to be."

"Can we still be friends?"

"I'd be disappointed if we weren't," Lana said as she stood up. "Would you like to join us? We're having coffee and pie and re-hashing the latest on Dan Smith."

"No. I think I'll go home. I'm just happy you're okay." As he walked to his car, Lana noticed that his shoulders were slumped more than usual.

"You're a hard woman to have to let go," Tony said, standing beside her.

"After I met you, I knew that what Ron and I had wasn't what I wanted in my marriage. I want passion. I want love. I want warmth and family. I want it all."

"Well, I'm sure the best man for that," Tony said, pulling her close against him and kissing her until her breathing was one with his.

# Epilogue

**Lana and her mom beamed at each other.** Lana's wedding dress was white, but her mom's was eggshell. They were about to walk down the aisle together in a double wedding.

"I can't believe I'm doing this," Alma said, looking down the aisle at Jim standing with Tony. They both had on tuxes, and both looked so handsome.

"Look at Tom," Lana giggled. "He looks so out of place in a tux, and he's head and shoulders taller than Jim." Tom Hoover was Jim's best man.

"He is one big guy," Alma agreed. "But isn't this whole thing so weird? It all started with us meeting to talk about Jenny and Hank's wedding. Tony was supposed to be Hank's best man, now Hank has wound up being Tony's. And Jenny's just sitting there as pregnant as can be and has never looked happier, and you and I are walking down the aisle!"

"Okay, Mom, we're on!" Lana said as the wedding march started. She and Alma had opted not to have any attendants. They wanted to walk down the aisle with their arms linked.

As Lana went toward Tony, his eyes locked with hers and never wavered. How had she ever gotten so lucky? she wondered. She'd found a man who loved her for who she was.

She'd found the best man for her.

# About the Author

**Pat Ballard lives in Nashville, TN.** She writes motivational romance novels to show that plus-size women can be just as sexy, romantic and exciting as their slim sisters.

Visit Pat on the web at www.patballard.com. Sign up for her free e-mail newsletter, *The Queen's Proclamation*, at www.pearlsong. com/pat_ballard.htm.

Find her other books published by Pearlsong Press—*Dangerous Curves Ahead: Short Stories, Wanted: One Groom, Nobody's Perfect, His Brother's Child, A Worthy Heir,* and *Abigail's Revenge*—at your favorite online and offline bookstores, as well as at www.pearlsong. com.

**The Queen of Rubenesque Romances** is also venturing into nonfiction! Look for her motivational book *10 Steps to Loving Your Body (No Matter What Size You Are)* in 2008.

**For news and updates about other Pearlsong Press** books and authors, subscribe to the free e-mail newsletter, *The Pearlsong Letter*, at www.pearlsong.com/subscribe.htm, or visit The Pearlsong Letter blog at www.pearlsongpress.com.